THE VALET

A TWISTY DOMESTIC THRILLER

BONNIE TRAYMORE

First Edition

Pathways Publishing

Print ISBN: 979-8-218-86893-2

ALSO BY BONNIE TRAYMORE

Killer Motives

Little Loose Ends

Head Case

The Stepfamily

The Guest House

The Bluff

A Little Getaway

The Unforgetting

Swipe

The Rich Guy's Wife

*For Addy and Everett, may you bring a little of the islands with
you, wherever life takes you*

PROLOGUE

ONE WEEK EARLIER

This should be one of the happiest days of Shayna McCarthy's life, except that it's not. Soon, she'll need to go back and face her friends. How long can she pretend to be using the bathroom?

But she's found a small corner of the resort to hide out while she attempts to determine how exactly a bout of cold feet comes on. Does it come in a flash and then disappear? Or is it more like a dull ache that you can sometimes ignore until you bang into a door and jolt it? What if you've experienced both?

Because the dull ache she's been suppressing for the last six months is nothing compared to the gut punch she received yesterday when she saw an old flame at Safeway. Her knees literally went weak, and that's never, ever happened with her fiancé.

The wedding is in a month and a half—mid-June—timed for when the children of her out-of-town guests will be finished with school. Honolulu is a long flight for many of them, and most people plan to make the most of the trip by adding a family vacation to the wedding. Shayna still has time to back out. It wouldn't be that bad. They could still come. Get that dream vacation.

It's not that she wants her ex back. He was trouble, and she doesn't want trouble. It's that she's not sure the guy she's marrying is the one. She tried to broach the subject with her maid of honor after getting a shot of tequila in her, but quickly realized her bachelorette getaway wasn't the time or the place. Instead, she pounded another shot and excused herself.

Now here she sits, searching for articles about cold feet.

A lone employee is hunkered down on the other side of the room, texting on his phone. He didn't notice her when she parked herself in the far corner of the resort, in an area that houses the conference rooms. Luckily, it's a weekend and they are all empty.

Shayna recognizes him from when they checked in yesterday, although they did not interact with each other. With his big, shiny head, he's hard to miss. Not a lot of hairless guys in this town.

Is he a bellman?

Or a valet, maybe?

It doesn't matter. What matters is that she is having second thoughts about her wedding. It probably doesn't help that this place is so romantic.

The elegant décor.

The beachfront setting and the fragrant breeze.

The multicolored sunset over a tranquil turquoise sea that she saw last night from her suite, watching couples stroll along hand in hand. She should have longed for Greg. Wished he were here with her. But that didn't happen.

As she reads through an article about the difference between pre-wedding jitters and cold feet on some bridal website she's landed on, she decides to put the issue on the back burner, go back to her friends, and have a good time.

This morning was spa treatments.

Now it's party time.

Tomorrow, she'll ask her bestie to stay behind for brunch and talk it through.

As she's about to get up to leave, a voice to the side of her interrupts, asking Shayna if they perhaps know each other from somewhere.

Rising from her seat, Shayna turns to see a person she does not recognize standing a few feet away from her club chair. "No," she says. "I don't think so." The person turns from her and walks in the opposite direction from where Shayna is headed.

Shayna goes on her way.

But as she starts her stroll back to the bar, a flash of memory hits.

"Oh, wait," she says, mostly to herself. She turns around, not able to recall the person's name. The face is vaguely familiar. She's not sure where from.

But when she looks over towards the seating area, the person is no longer there. Just the lone bellman. Or valet. Or whoever he is, still glued to his phone, oblivious.

Strange.

ONE

JOHNNY

"I've got this one," I yell out to the guys.

Yup. I remember this guy from last week. Total douchebag. Probably a crappy tipper, but I was off duty when he got his car back.

Not a tourist.

I think he's new in town.

Perfect.

He tosses the key card to me, like I might give him leprosy if he places it in my outstretched palm. I hook the ticket to the key ring, rip off the tag, and hold it out. He plucks it from my fingers and shoves it in his pants pocket.

"Don't scratch it," he says.

I fight the urge to give him a dirty look. Instead, I flash him my Johnny Boy smile. An obsequious mask I've perfected over the years. That's what some people call me. Johnny Boy. I hate it and love it in equal measure. But that's too complicated a notion to dwell on now.

Hopping in the douchebag's Roadster, I watch as he struts over towards the hotel in his khakis and polo shirt. High-end

Tesla drivers are the worst. Smug pricks who think they can justify their conspicuous consumption because they're saving the environment.

Do you know that one EV battery can take as much energy to produce as driving a car for tens of thousands of miles? And don't get me started on the lithium and the cobalt and the human and environmental tolls they take.

Some days, when it's slow, I've got time on my hands. I listen to a lot of podcasts. I know stuff. Stuff that would surprise you. Most of it I keep to myself, because if people think I'm stupid, they'll underestimate me. That tends to work in my favor.

Tesla Guy veers right, away from the hotel entrance and towards the restaurant. Stalling, I try to get a glimpse of who he's meeting. The more information I can glean, the better. It's right before peak lunchtime. Not too crowded, so I can afford to take it slow.

I spot Danny Yamamoto, over in the direction Tesla Guy is headed. Is he meeting Yamamoto? Yamamoto's a local real estate developer. Good guy. Great tipper. I'd feel sorry for him if he was meeting with this guy. He's the type to screw you over, I can tell just by looking at him.

Nope. He passes up Danny. That's a relief.

Then I notice a slender woman with long, dark hair. I can only see her in profile, dressed like a real estate agent but with the demeanor of someone on a first date. The guy walks towards her and offers her a wave. Maybe it's a dating app meet-up. They smile and shake hands. Hard to tell if it's business or pleasure.

A short tap on a horn startles me.

I'm holding up the line to the parking garage, so I start moving.

People rarely beep their horns here in Honolulu, and if

they do, it's only a slight tap. A gentle reminder. Not like New York City. I lived there for a year, back in the day, when I wanted to be an actor. I got used to it. You'd think, growing up in Honolulu, the noise would have driven me crazy. But I grew to appreciate it. Leaning on the horn was a way of blowing off steam, I came to realize. Like letting out a primal scream, but one that didn't torque your vocal cords. We have a lot of road rage here now. I wonder, if we leaned on the horn more, would it help?

I pull into the parking structure, but of course, I don't have to go far because the Roadster gets a prime spot.

This works for me, though. The car behind me is a gas guzzler. A Nissan SUV, so my coworker Leo has to take it up another level or two. This gives me a few minutes, which is all I need.

People try to be safe, taking their house keys off the ring, as if we have time to go to a locksmith and make a copy of their key. I know that's happened in the past, but what are the odds? It would have to be a very slow establishment, or one of those situations where the valet driver has to roam around the block looking for street parking, not a garage situation like we have.

Even then, I can't imagine it happening here, with the traffic jams we have. Much too risky, and it's a small town. If I went to get keys made time after time, someone would put two and two together. So, relax people. It's not that big a risk, at least in Honolulu, to give your entire key chain to the valet driver.

But it's not without risk, valeting your car. I've heard of valet drivers taking joy rides, cracking up cars. Before GPS and valet mode, that happened more often. Or scratching them and not saying anything. It's not like people check before they drive away. I'd never do anything like that, and neither would any of the drivers here. It's a luxury property. We've got class—and oversight.

Most people are trusting, and that makes me happy. They leave valuables in the car in plain sight. If they are extra careful or the suspicious type, they'll lock stuff in the glove box, if the car has a lock. Some of them don't anymore. It's kind of insulting when people do this right in front of us, like they think we're stupid. If your stuff went missing while we had your car, we'd obviously be the prime suspects.

You'd be surprised what you can glean from the contents of a glove box. One time, I found a woman's cancer diagnosis. She was rude to me, but I let it slide after I saw that. Cancer sucks, that's for sure. Another time, I found a stack of hundreds, and I thought it was a setup. I didn't take the money, of course. I'm not that stupid.

This guy's glove box is inaccessible to me. He's got it in valet mode. Hard to top a Tesla if you want security. The interior of the car is pretty clean, which doesn't surprise me. He looks like a neat freak. Close-cropped salt and pepper hair. Clean-shaven face. Large hands that belong to a white-collar worker, with nails all trimmed to the same length.

But he does have a folder on the seat. Maybe he forgot it when he rushed over to meet the lady. I flip it open and page through it. It's a rental agreement. Lucky me.

Derek Anderson.

Renting a house in Aina Haina.

Not too far.

I grab my phone to snap a photo, but Leo startles me.

I slam the folder shut, just in time.

"Hey," Leo says as I'm getting out of the car.

Leo shoots me a look, as if asking why I'm not already back at the valet stand, since he had to drive further and he's already to my car, so I quick put my phone to my ear and pretend I'm on a call.

"I can't talk now, babe! I told you. I'm working." Then I wait a second and continue. "It's not *that* slow. I gotta bounce." Shoving my phone in my pocket, I say to Leo, "Women."

Leo rolls his eyes in solidarity.

His wife is a total nag.

I offer him a shrug.

That was close. Too close.

So close that I didn't get a photo of Tesla Guy's address.

TWO
JOHNNY

Janice looks great today. I can't put my finger on what's different about her from her good days to her bad days, but she's the kind of woman who can go from a nine to a six inside of twenty-four hours. It's merely an observation. I'm no less attracted to her on an off day. It's all about pheromones, and on a chemical level, we work.

It's not the make-up, because unless we're going out somewhere special, she's pretty consistent about it: eyeliner, mascara, a light shade of coral gracing her bountiful lips. I'm thinking it's the quality of her sleep. She looks well rested today, with that feisty gleam in her eye. She flashes me a smile that sets me on fire. I lean in and try to cop a feel, but she pushes me away.

"Tell me about the target first," Janice says, as she crosses her arms. She loves a good mark, which explains the look in her eye, which is clearly not for me.

We're at her one-bedroom apartment, which she rents in Kaimuki, a dense neighborhood with narrow, winding back streets where cars dodge each other and try to avoid head-on collisions. The main drag is a mix of trendy bohemian and old school Honolulu. She lives in an iconic circular building, in a unit that's seen better days.

I roll my eyes. "What's there to tell? I told you everything I know. Tesla-driving douchebag. Lives in Aina Haina. FOB mainland, I'm sure."

"We don't say that anymore."

"Douchebag?" I ask.

She narrows her eyes at me. "Mainland."

"Right. FOB *the continent*. Better?"

Janice is uber PC, and this isn't the first time she's schooled me on this point. A lot of people still say mainland, especially around tourists, and it's hard to break the habit. But my girl tells me it has a postcolonial connotation, so I make a mental note to try harder, at least around Janice.

"Better," she says. "What makes you think he's new in town?"

"Just a hunch."

A look of resignation flashes across her face. "Well, your hunch was right. But he's renting the house. Looks like he got here a few weeks before he got the rental nailed down. The car's leased. Maybe he's a poseur."

Janice is a real estate agent, which comes in very handy. She's got access to information that people like me don't. We make a good team, her and me. A benevolent Bonnie and Clyde. We're into victimless crimes. The people we target have lots of insurance, and we all know those companies are a total scam. Don't blame us. Blame wealth inequality. We're just trying to get by.

I shrug. "What difference does that make? We're not after his car."

"How do you know it was real?" Janice asks.

"I know a Yacht Master when I see one," I tell her.

My dad was a jeweler. I know my watches. And the Yacht Master is popular around here. Top of the line Rolex, worth over twenty grand. Janice likes to play the role of devil's advocate, though, and that's usually a good thing.

"It's not an easy piece to lift," she points out. "He probably wears it every day."

See? This is what I have to deal with.

But like I said, it's not horrible. She forces me to think through the potential pitfalls. "There's more where that came from. I'm sure of it," I tell her. "Don't be a buzz kill."

"I think we should wait for a woman. Guys don't tend to have a lot of jewelry."

Janice points out what she's hammered into me on numerous occasions. Target women, decked out for the evening. Wearing their fancy dress jewelry, the kinds of pieces that won't be noticed for months after they go missing.

"Let's do some more research. I have a good feeling about this guy. He seems shady. The kind of guy who keeps a lot of cash around the house."

"Shady? That's exactly what we don't need. Let's find someone else."

"Calm down, woman. Let's not be rash about this. Tell me about the house."

Our business model is pretty simple. Find people with high-quality jewelry that's not one of a kind. Target single-family homes in the suburbs that are easy to break into, so that eliminates the super-rich. No Royal Drive or Kahala Avenue homes for us. They have security systems and cameras. Luxury high-rises are a possibility if Janice can get us into the building when there's a vacant listing. We aim for jewelry, but if we spot something valuable on the fly, we'll grab it. I have a fence for the jewelry, courtesy of my dad. I wasn't planning on following in his footsteps, but then I met Janice.

She tells me about the property, and it sounds perfect. Tucked away in a suburb, not too high-end, although in this area, even fixers go for a million dollars. Single-wall construction. Jalousie window panels which are easy to lift out of the frames. Dated. As a rental, it probably doesn't have much security.

"What do we have to lose?" I ask. "Let's try it. He's single, as far as we know."

"Good looking?" she asks.

I grab her by the ass and pull her into me. "Why? You thinking of trading me in?"

"Not on your life," she says.

And she means it. I'm not insecure about Janice, or about women in general. I've got a secret weapon, and I know how to use it.

She placates me with a steamy kiss, then asks me again about the guy. "Scale of one to ten?"

I shrug, because I don't know how to answer this. I think about saying something like *I'm not into guys*, but that might not land well. She's sensitive about these matters, and I don't want to come off as homophobic.

"Why are you dwelling on this?" I ask.

"We don't need someone who gets a lot of action. Someone who's likely to have women over the house all the time. What if he's seeing a bunch of them, and one of them stakes out the house, trying to check out their competition? Someone could see us."

I give her a tickle. "Are you speaking from experience here?"

"Stop," she says. "You know what I mean. I don't want to go to prison."

"Neither do I. But you need to trust me on this one, babe. We've targeted enough women. We don't want to be gender biased. I know how you hate that. This guy deserves it. Think of it as a public service." I flash her a smirk.

She rolls her eyes, then tilts her head to one side. After a pause, she says, "Okay, maybe you have a point. We don't want to be too predictable."

"That's my girl," I say. "Now speaking of getting some action ..."

I pull her in for a kiss. She obliges for a few minutes, fondling my smooth head. She has a thing about it, which works for me. But then she stops us in our tracks.

"Later," she says, pushing me away. "First, we need a plan."

THREE

JOHNNY

I have a sinking feeling that Leo suspects something. It's just a hunch. It's not like he said anything, but I have a suspicion that he saw me looking through the folder. We rotate, and it was Leo's turn to grab a car when Derek Anderson came for his Tesla. I sort of cut the line so I could find out his address. Coupled with the way Leo eyed me earlier when I was sitting in the car, I'm thinking maybe we should cool it for a while.

At fifty-one, Leo's nearly two decades my elder and not too quick on the draw. It was hot, so I tried to couch it as a humanitarian gesture.

"I got it," I said to Leo. "It's boiling hot out there."

Leo nodded, like he appreciated the fact that he could stay in the shade, near the valet stand. But he had to grab the next one, so what I said didn't make any sense at all, which makes me think he could suspect something.

The guy actually gave me a pretty good tip, but he didn't thank me. Didn't say a word, in fact. I did get a better look at the dark-haired woman he met for lunch when she was waiting for her car, which Leo retrieved shortly after I delivered the Tesla.

I think it was a business meeting, or else a very bad first date. Tesla Guy split first, which doesn't seem very gentlemanly if it was a date, given that he didn't wait for her. Maybe she went to the ladies' room. If my lady was in the restroom, I'd wait for her, that's for sure.

But back to Leo. I'll talk to Janice about taking a hiatus, or even stopping our side hustle altogether. We've been lucky so far, and one thing I know about luck is it eventually runs out. We should probably quit while we're ahead.

Walking from the parking garage to the hotel where I work, I take a moment to appreciate the beauty. Most days, I don't. But today it hits me, like it must when a tourist arrives for the first time. Or when Captain Cook and his shipmates stepped on shore, snapping the islands out of centuries of isolation, opening them up to disease, debauchery, and development, kind of in that order. Not that I'm complaining. I stay out of politics. It's just, those are the facts.

The Grand Royal Hotel sits on a peninsula that juts out a bit on the Kahala Coast, near Royal Place, next to some of the most expensive real estate in the world, grandfathered in as a commercial property in a residential zone. It's a boutique property on a small beach that sits in front of a tranquil sea, not great for swimming or surfing because of the coral, but good for wading or a quick dip to cool off on a hot day.

A luxury spa and two oceanfront restaurants make it popular with the locals. It was built in the sixties, in the era of postwar prosperity and affordable jet travel, a Honolulu classic that's changed hands many times but has retained its old-world charm. Elegant and understated, it's nothing like the megaresorts that dot the neighbor islands.

I'm kind of old school, and I think I would have liked it

better back in the day, in another era. Before social media. Before the internet. Before electric cars. This place reminds me of simpler times. It soothes me, which is probably why I stay, even though I want more out of life.

"Hey," I say to Tina, the woman working behind the valet counter this morning, but she barely looks up at me. She's reading something on her phone. It's slow now. Nothing much happening yet on this classic Honolulu morning. Trades at ten to fifteen, temp in the high seventies. Perfect weather, which I grew to appreciate more after spending time in other states.

There aren't too many women valet drivers. I know because I've done this job in other cities. It's a good skill to fall back on, and even though I wanted more from my life, still do, I can find work anywhere. When I lived in LA for a year, the company I worked for made an effort to recruit more women, but with very little success.

But you will see women working behind the valet stand, like Tina. They don't park the cars. They stay behind and direct the flow, or make change if a customer needs it. Maybe it's so they don't melt their make-up in the heat? It seems boring to me. I like to be busy.

I could kick myself for being such a good salesman. At first, Janice wasn't too interested in going after Derek Anderson. But by the end of our discussion, she was more excited about it than I was, which resulted in a quite satisfying evening. Like I said, Janice gets pretty charged up when we land on a new target. The scratches on my back sting a little, but it was worth it. It's going to be hard to convince her to retire our little side hustle.

Tina's still glued to her phone. It's unlike her. She's usually pretty friendly.

"Got a hot one on your dating app?" I chide.

Tina and her husband split up last year, and last month she told me she was putting herself out there again. Trying one of those apps. She's lost a little weight, but she's still what I'd call full-figured. Attractive. Nice complexion. She could get dates if she wanted to.

Tina shakes her head. "No. I'm giving that a rest," she says. "I'm reading about the woman."

"What woman?"

"Didn't you hear the news?"

"Can you be more specific?"

"That missing woman, from last week? Shayna McCarthy?"

"Oh yeah," I say. "What about her?"

Sounded to me like a runaway bride who didn't wait for her wedding day to take off. Engaged, they said. Wedding in a month or so. But one of her friends said on the news she was having second thoughts.

"She was found murdered. Dumped in the Kawainui Marsh."

"Murdered? Shit. I figured she split on him. It's probably the fiancé. Wasn't she thinking about calling off the wedding?"

Tina shrugs. "Nothing about him or any suspects yet," she says. "They didn't come out and say it was a homicide, but what else would it be?"

"Maybe she had a stroke while she was out walking. It's a popular hiking spot. Doesn't seem like a great place to dump a body."

"The article said it was a 'suspicious death.' You know how the cops are. The less information they release, the more worried I get. If they think it's a serial killer, they won't want to tip him off with details or get everyone all excited. Remember the Honolulu Strangler?"

I tell her I don't, and she gives me the rundown on Honolulu's only serial killer, back in the eighties. It took quite a few bodies before they started to call it a serial killer, she tells me.

"What are the odds, Tina? It's always the husband. Or the boyfriend. Isn't that what they say? She wanted out of the relationship. She turned up dead. You do the math."

"I guess," Tina says.

"So, what does this have to do with you and the dating app?"

"Nothing. I just decided I wasn't ready. And this dead woman isn't helping."

Tina can't seem to take her eyes off the woman, and my co-worker's pained expression draws my eyes to her phone screen. I see a woman around thirty. Long, dark hair and a bright smile on her face that reaches the eyes, the same photo that's been plastered all over the media for the past few days. You can tell she's looking at someone she trusts. I wonder if the boyfriend took it. If so, he obviously fooled her because it's the look of a woman who's comfortable and content.

"She was here last week," Tina says. "I remember her. All excited about her bachelorette weekend with her girls. I was like that once." She lets out a long sigh as she shakes her head. "Seems like a lifetime ago."

Tina never told me that her ex was violent, but I got the feeling she was scared of him. That it wasn't an amicable break-up. Once, she came to work with a bruise on her arm in the shape of a thumb. She played it down. Said she'd banged it on a door frame when she was tipsy. Another time, he showed up here looking for her, but she wasn't working that day. He got in my face. Accused me of lying. I had to call security.

Tina felt embarrassed, and we all tried to assure her it wasn't her fault. Told her we had her back. But she's the type to blame herself, which is probably how she got herself into a situation like that to begin with. Too sweet and trusting for this world.

"Look, Tina," I say. "There's a lot of good guys out there. When you're ready, I've got a friend—"

She holds up a hand. "It's not like that, Johnny. Don't worry about me. I can take care of myself," she says. The tough girl expression on her face is at odds with her Mini Mouse voice.

The thought of it makes me sick, preying on a woman. I'm a bigger guy, not tall but broad, but I don't act like one. Coupled with my shiny, hairless head, I can come off as menacing. But my dad always taught me that bigger guys have a responsibility to be gentle, like he was with my mom. Mom needed that, he told me, after what she'd been through. I wanted to be like my dad. The kind of guy who would try to defuse a situation, to a point. He also taught me to keep the anger under wraps for as long as possible, so that when you did need to let loose, they'd never see it coming.

It got me into some trouble when I was younger, because I present like I'm docile. Like someone you don't have to worry about. Someone who's timid or will back down. I won't. But that's probably why I got the nickname Johnny Boy. My demeanor works to my advantage, though, because the tough guys underestimate me. My ferocity catches them off guard.

But with women? Never. I've got a soft spot for the ladies, and I'm more the type to defend a woman, within reason. One time, I was at a dive bar in Chinatown, and this guy was getting rough with a girl. It seemed like they knew each other, but I still stepped in. Told him to leave her alone. I've got a short fuse with wife beaters.

Well, long story short, we ended up in a brawl, and he nearly bit off my ear. I had to get stitches and antibiotics, which really screwed up my stomach. I messed him up pretty good, too, and we had to go to court. So, I learned to pick my battles. Even when I saw him again and he taunted me. Called me a pussy, I didn't take the bait. If that hadn't happened, I might have gotten more in the face of Tina's ex. But I can't lose my job, and I don't like to call attention to myself in that way if I can help it, so I let security handle it.

"We've all got your back around here, Tina. You got good security at home?" I ask.

She looks up and gives me a hard stare: "I've got a nine-millimeter."

My eyes widen. "Props, Tina."

"I told you, Johnny. You don't need to worry about me," she says. She returns her gaze to the murder victim. An edge to her delivery tells me she doesn't want my pity.

Maybe Tina's not too sweet for this world, after all.

"Good for you," I say.

But she's still staring down at the photo, as if it holds some clues.

"Not too good for her, though," she says.

All I can do is nod.

"I don't think it's the fiancé," she adds.

"Why not?"

"Just a hunch," she says. "I think it's something worse."

FOUR

LANI

It's just before dawn when Lani Lum heads down the elevator to go outside for her run, clutching a bag of garbage. Soon the bell dings, and she's at the lobby level. Although it's a safe neighborhood and a secure building, it usually sends a chill up her spine when she ducks into the dark room off the lobby that houses the dumpster.

This time is no exception.

There's something eerie about it. The way it takes a few seconds for the lights to come on, leaving her imagination to run wild in the pitch dark. It smells of rotting food and mustiness, although the dumpster is relatively empty at the moment.

Tossing the bag into the metal bin, she lets go of the plastic handle and listens as the bag lands with a loud thud. She's put some glass bottles in there rather than the recycling bin, and a pang of guilt stabs her. She's been too busy, or lazy, to wash them out, and Lani doesn't want to attract pests. They don't empty the recycling often, and the sugar from the cranberry juice container surely would. She's not sure about the pickle jar or the wine bottle. She vows to do better next week, when things settle down at work.

The lights flicker on as she's about to turn and dash back out, but that's not to be her fate. It all happens in a flash:

A firm hand clamps around her nose and mouth.

An arm presses tight against her right side, rendering her legs and arm useless.

A wet cloth cradled in its palm forces a gag as some liquid seeps into her mouth.

A sharp jab to her thigh demands her attention.

What was that?

From the left, another arm encircles her, rendering her remaining limb useless.

Lani barely has time to register what's happening, and for a moment, she holds on to the hope that this is a bad dream. She'll wake up in bed, have a laugh at herself and her vivid imagination, and get on with her day.

IT'S NOT A DREAM, she soon realizes.

She can't breathe.

Weakness washes over her.

I should be fighting.

Why am I not fighting?

Then it clicks.

The sharp prick.

Some kind of drug?

Struggling to stay conscious, she musters up enough energy to wiggle her right arm and jut her elbow back into her captor's torso, but it's useless.

As she surrenders to the darkness, one last thought floats by.

Why me?

FIVE

JOHNNY

"I think we should cool it for a while on the side hustle," I say to Janice.

We're at my place this time, and she's just arrived from a showing. I own a small condo in the Diamond Head area, on a less pricey circle with a bunch of low-rise cinder block complexes built in the fifties and sixties, nestled at the base of Honolulu's most iconic landmark, which hikes up our square foot price.

Today, the jagged ridges of Diamond Head, a dormant volcano, pierce the afternoon sky. White cotton balls dot its peaks. It's pretty damn nice, if I do say so myself, admiring the view from my lanai before turning back towards Janice, who is fixing herself a mojito in my kitchen. This isn't the worst place in the world to be struggling.

Our "affordable" units sit behind Kapi'olani Park, a former horse racing track from the days of the monarchy, peppered with flowering shower trees and enormous, vine-covered banyan trees that entertain kids who swing and climb, and shade picnickers from the blazing sun. It's sprawling, and there's even an outdoor stadium, where I've spent more than a few evenings rocking out or swaying, depending on the headliner.

Behind our units sit the multi-million-dollar single-family homes that house our superrich. I bought the condo nearly a decade ago, scraping together a down payment from a military death benefit when my mother passed away, most of which went to my dad. When I say small, I mean small. It's under five hundred square feet, so we hardly ever hang out here, but at least it's mine, as long as I can keep up the mortgage payments, which are high right now because I got hooked into a variable-rate loan. I could lose this place if things don't turn around. Because of the insurance rate hikes, our maintenance fees have doubled, and the hotel has been slower than normal, so my tip income is down.

Still, I'm not itching to go to prison.

"COOL IT? WHY?" Janice says, planting her hands on her hips.

I explain to her about Leo and that I think he might suspect something.

Throwing her hands up, she says, "And you say I worry too much?"

Expecting this, I continue, placing a firm hand on her shoulder. As much as Janice likes to assert herself, feisty gal that she is, I know from experience that she likes a firm hand once in a while, both literally and figuratively.

"We've been lucky so far, Janice. And sooner or later, it'll run out. You know this."

She rolls her eyes and asks me if I've seen Leo since the incident.

"No," I say. "I'll see him tomorrow."

"Let's see what happens, okay? See if we can get a read on him? If he does anything to make you think he's on to you, then we'll forget it."

She looks up at me, not quite batting her eyes, but close. She's hard to resist, and relationships are all about compromise, so I agree. Even if Leo doesn't say something that gets my hackles up, I can still tell Janice he did. How would she even know? A little white lie to save us from prison. I shouldn't have let her lead me down this road to begin with.

This placates her for the time being, and we move on to other topics. She brings up the murdered woman, Shayna McCarthy. Like Tina, Janice is into true crime, so she's following the story.

"It's the fiancé," I say. "Don't worry about it."

"Why would I worry about it?" she says.

I give her a recap of my conversation with my coworker Tina, and how she thought it might be a serial killer.

Her nose scrunches up as she tilts her head to the side. She's got a cute little nose that looks like it belongs on a ten-year-old. "Serial killer? That seems a little premature."

"That's what I said."

"It's always the husband," she says.

"I said that, too."

"See? That's why we're perfect for each other. And you know why you're perfect for me?" She places her arms around my neck, standing on her tiptoes to do so. I'm not that tall, but she's downright tiny.

"Why is that?"

"Because you'd never hurt a woman, Johnny. You're a protector. You've got a protector's instinct. That's what I love about you." She squeezes my bicep, which is formidable, if I do say so myself.

I lift weights a little, but not as much as you would think. I had a friend when I was younger, thin guy. He had a lot of trouble building muscle, even with me coaching him. I realized then that I have the type of body that builds muscle easily. I'm lucky that way.

But I can also put on weight in a flash, so I have to watch what I eat. That guy? He scarfed food down like a sumo wrestler and never gained a pound. Still, it works for Janice, and we both know that if she wants to hit this guy in Aina Haina, I'm probably going to give in. But I'll feel out Leo and take it from there.

The first person we targeted was exactly the type of mark Janice wanted. A woman in her sixties. A divorcee with a lot of insurance and no money problems, as far as we could tell. She was a regular at the spa. Came monthly. A lousy tipper, but on the friendly side. We never, ever target hotel guests. That would be way too obvious, and it might get one of the house-keeping girls in trouble. The hotel has a membership program for locals. For a hefty annual fee, they can use the pool and sign for their meals, like a country club. Regulars are good to target because they're predictable.

This woman seemed to check all the boxes. She didn't wear much jewelry on spa days, but she also came for lunch with her lady friends from time to time, and that's when I noticed her. High-quality, unremarkable jewelry, not one of a kind. Classic, with large stones that would be easy to sell. Plus, she had a regular spa appointment, and she lived alone. We could kind of time it for when she'd be out of the house.

It was easy to break into her home. It was in Kahala, but not on the ocean, or makai, side. Perched halfway up a steep hill on the mauka, or mountain, side, with a high metal fence that partially blocked the view of the house from the street. She didn't have a safe, and her jewelry sat in a mango wood box on her dresser. It almost felt too easy.

Janice wanted to take the whole box, but I said no. I went through and found a pair of diamond earrings with large, high-quality stones and an emerald necklace with a plain chain, and that was supposed to be that. But then Janice rifled through her underwear drawer and found a few antique-looking pieces. A bracelet and matching earrings. Solid gold with large gemstones. She wanted to take them, too.

I put my foot down. "No way," I said. "Too one-of-a-kind."

It was a decisive no, and she didn't argue with me.

That's what I mean about Janice liking a firm hand.

But here's the thing. I could have taken the pieces apart and sold the stones. They were valuable. But they looked to me like heirlooms. Like something with sentimental value. Something the insurance money couldn't replace, and I didn't want that on my conscience. I'm not religious, but I believe in karma, and I'm a little superstitious. I didn't want to tempt fate. So, we left them.

Instead, we took her solid silver flatware and her gold bangles. We were in and out inside of fifteen minutes.

I think back on the conversation with Janice that finally prompted me to go along with her plan. Her real estate business, she complained, was tanking. It wasn't her fault. Big tech and online listing services were driving agents into bankruptcy. Commissions were no longer a given in real estate sales. She'd managed to supplement her income with the occasional sticky finger, but since the advent of digital lockboxes that record who comes and goes and when, that sideline was no longer a viable option, so she suggested that we handpick a few of my customers and go after them.

It made sense to me at the time, and she's right about big tech. I never made it very far on my quest to be an actor. A few day player roles here and on the mainland. Work as an extra, which is hardly worth the effort. But for a while, I had a side hustle doing voice-overs. That's dwindled, too, with AI on the scene. The cards are stacked against people like Janice and me, and eventually, human beings in general.

I went with it. And if I'm being honest, there's a part of me that likes living on the edge. My girl didn't have to push me that hard. The thrill of getting away with something. Having a secret I hide from the world. Having a secret like that to share with Janice, which is kind of hot.

Maybe it's in my genes. My father was a small business owner, which is tough here in Honolulu. If you think rents are bad for homes and apartments, try looking at commercial property. Online jewelry sales sliced into his market share.

There's your big tech again.

He kept afloat doing repairs and selling to his regulars, an aging clientele that was not going to last forever. I don't know when or how he started selling stolen pieces, I only know when he got caught.

I was a senior in high school. He made a deal with the prosecutor and got a pretty light sentence. Then he cashed out and moved off island, which was probably a smart move. He had to give up some names to get the deal. He left me all his tools, though, along with a very sick mom. Because I worked summers and after school at the store, I learned enough about the business to pull off what we're doing.

With college no longer an option, I finished high school, moved in with my tutu after Mom died, saved up money working as a valet driver, and blew it trying to get my acting career off the ground. I suppose that's a weak excuse for the choices I've made, but it's the only one I can give you. I still have a pile of credit card debt. But I have some equity in my condo and maybe a month's worth of expenses in my checking account. One more score and we could cash out and move to Vegas, where our money would go a lot further.

Janice loves Vegas

I'll take Leo's skin temperature. If he's cool, we'll go after Tesla Guy. He deserves it. That'll be the deal I make with Janice.

One more score, and then we're out.

SIX

JOHNNY

Today is voggy.

My eyes water and itch as the silent sulfur gas spewing out of Kilauea Volcano on the Big Island, a hundred miles away, permeates my corneas. When the trades stop and we get Kona winds, the toxins float in our direction and hover over us like a mushroom cloud until the trades come back and blow it all out to sea.

I've only been here two hours. Already it's practically intolerable, and I have to be out here all damn day. That would be one plus of moving to Vegas. No vog.

"What's the matter, Johnny Boy? Did Janice dump you?" Leo says.

"Funny guy, you. The freaking volcano," I say, rubbing my eyes.

"Doesn't bother me," Leo replies. "Maybe it's your imagination."

It's not my imagination. Lots of people are bothered by vog. I knew a woman who had to move away because it made her migraines worse. But I don't say any of this to Leo. It's not worth the trouble.

So far, if Leo suspects anything, he's not letting on about it, which leads me to believe he doesn't. If he did, he's more the type to try to get a piece of it than the type to turn me in. He's also a decent guy, so he might let it go. He hates wise ass rich guys as much as I do. I could always lie to Janice and say I got a weird vibe, but I'm starting to like the idea of using it as a compromise strategy. I'm ready to leave, but I want her to come with me.

I grew up here, and I suppose I'm considered local, but that's been tempered by my time in other states, so I know I won't mind leaving, especially on days like today, with my eyes burning as much as they are. I'm not sure about Janice. She's more local than I am.

That's as far as I usually go in defining people in terms of ethnicity here: local or not local. Janice and Leo are local. Tesla guy is FOB mainland—*continent*—and he'll never be local, no matter how long he stays.

I dated an Italian woman in New York. A real one, from Italy. She took issue with the way Americans would proudly proclaim *I'm Italian*—or Irish or Vietnamese or Portuguese; you get the idea. *You're all Americans. Why do you pretend that you are not?*

I grew to agree with her sentiment, which is why I don't think of people in terms of their heritage. Me, I'm a mix, and I've been told all my life what its components were, but when I got my genetic testing back, it didn't even match up with our family tree. So, my dad is local, my mom is not. That's my story. She came here with the military to escape a toxic family situation and met my father, and we lost her way too early. There's more to that story, of course, but I don't want to dwell on it. Makes me sad, and generally speaking, I'm a happy person.

Honolulu, like New York, is a melting pot of cultures and ethnicities, and I found the cities to be surprisingly similar. Rich, poor, old, young, all sharing the same public spaces, whether they be beaches or parks or benches. You can't hide from the have-nots like you can in California. I bet the Tesla guy is from California. Rich people there are insufferable.

Which gets me back to the matter at hand. I'll talk to Janice tonight, and I'll try to make the deal. One last job, then we cash out and go to Vegas.

"VEGAS? Why would I want to move to Vegas?" Janice says.

This isn't going the way I envisioned it. We're at her place, as per usual. She doesn't like to scavenge around for parking near me, and generally speaking, I go to her. I don't mind too much. I like my place the way it is, and if we hung there more, she'd probably try harder to put her stamp on it.

"You love Vegas," I say.

"For a weekend. Not to live there. All that glitz twenty-four seven? I'd lose my mind."

"We wouldn't live on the strip, Janice. We'd be in a suburb. In a nice house. Or a townhouse, with a pool and spa and all the amenities you love so much."

She lets out a long sigh. "I get what you're saying. But it's so bleak there. I need more beauty. How about Lake Tahoe? At least that's scenic."

California is out of the question, but the Nevada side may be okay. I'm not big on altitude, but I could adjust.

Compromise.

Or I could get her to look at the Reno area. It's close enough to Tahoe. Affordable. For now, I leave it.

"Tahoe, eh? We could look into it. Nevada's pretty good for taxes."

"Let me ask around. See what the real estate market's like in Nevada. What would you do there?" she asks.

It's a fair question. I suppose I'd need to be near an upscale resort if I'm going to make any money valeting cars, although I'd rather do something else. Something more related to acting. Most of all, I want to get out of the jewelry business before we get arrested.

"Don't worry about me," I say. "I always land on my feet."

Janice purses her lips and stares off into space for a bit. "Okay," she says. "I could use a change. It's an adventure. It could be fun."

"So that's the plan? We hit this guy, and then we're out?"

"That's the plan," she agrees.

Janice is a curious woman. Nothing like the others I've been with. Even after two years, she's never even hinted at marriage or moving in together. Still, if I'm asking her to move away with me, I should probably get a ring and pop the question.

But what if she says no?

Where would that leave us?

I've certainly got a lot to think about, so I prioritize and focus on something I can control.

"So, let's figure out when this hit will go down," I say.

We get to work on a plan.

SEVEN
JOHNNY

"I told you I had a bad feeling," Tina says to me as I shuffle up to the valet stand. Funny. That's the exact same thing I said to Janice when we broke into Derek Anderson's house two nights ago and found nothing of value to steal.

"A bad feeling about what?" I ask.

"Didn't you hear?" My coworker looks at me like there's a nuclear missile headed for Honolulu for real this time.

"Hear what?" I ask.

"Another woman's missing. That's two women inside of two weeks. Long, dark hair. Around the same age as the runaway bride. I told you. It's a serial killer. I know it is."

"Don't jump to conclusions," I say. "It could be a coincidence. What are the cops saying?"

Tina shrugs. "Not much."

"Maybe the media's jumping on it to get some clickbait. Trying to make it into something it isn't. People love a good serial killer story. The cops brought the fiancé in for questioning on that other case, didn't they?"

Tina lets out a huff. "Easy for you to say, Johnny."

"What's easy for me to say?"

"You're not a woman with long, dark hair. If it is a serial killer, he's not after you."

"It's not a serial killer," I say.

"Unless it is," Tina barks at me.

Leo steps up to the valet stand. "What's all the commotion?" he asks.

"Oh," I tell him. "Tina thinks we've got a serial killer in town."

"I don't watch the news," Leo says.

"You're just as bad as Johnny," Tina says. "You can afford to not watch the news."

"What's that supposed to mean?" Leo asks.

I tell him, "It means you're not a woman with long, dark hair."

Leo's brow furrows. "Huh?"

"Another woman's missing," Tina tells Leo. "Lani Lum. A woman who looks like the woman they found murdered, dumped in the Kawainui marsh."

"Oh, I heard about the woman in the marsh," Leo says. "I thought they brought the boyfriend in."

Shrugging, I say to Leo, "That's what I said."

Tina holds out a photo to me. "Will you two look at this?" she says.

When my eyes hit the phone screen, my jaw drops.

Tina's face scrunches up as she examines me. "What? What is it, Johnny? Do you know her?"

Seeing my expression, Leo glances down at the screen and there's... nothing. I'm about to tell them it's the same woman who was with Tesla Guy. The woman whose car Leo retrieved. I'm about to bat Leo on the arm and say, "Hey, dimwit, that's the girl!"

But then I stop myself.

Because if Leo retrieved her car and he doesn't remember her, how will it look if I do? Leo already seemed a little suspicious, the way I lingered inside the Roadster that day. How would I explain the fact that I stared at her long enough to remember her face?

What if Tina thinks *I'm* the serial killer?

So, I catch myself.

"No," I say. "But she does look a little like the runaway bride, I'll give you that."

"You know who else she looks like?" Tina says.

Leo lets out a breath.

I offer her a hesitant shrug.

The woman looks a little like Tina, and we all see it.

"Don't worry," I try to assure her. "It'll be fine."

I KNOW I said that breaking into a house with jalousie windows was easy, but not if they are so rusted that the metal frame has fused to the glass, which was the case with Derek Anderson's rental. I told Janice we should forget it. That I had a bad feeling.

"There's no such thing as a bad feeling," she said. "I don't believe in that."

She took out her nail kit and picked open the back door lock before I could give her a better reason to abandon our mission.

Once we were in, we looked around for the Yacht Master, but Janice was right. He probably wears the watch all the time, and it was nowhere to be found. He had a Garmin, but that's not worth much, and it's connected to GPS, recording all those bodily functions people love to monitor these days. Totally trackable.

Hard pass.

Other than that, we found a class ring from Stanford and a pair of diamond cufflinks, which would be very hard to sell in Honolulu. Who wears diamond cufflinks these days anyway? The stones were too small to bother with, and I wonder why he even brought them here. It's clear that he's got another residence somewhere. It's a furnished rental, and he has roughly the amount of stuff you'd bring for a two-week hotel stay.

Apparently, he has a lady friend. We spotted some women's costume jewelry in a bathroom drawer, along with mascara, eyeliner, and a tube of lipstick. Oddly, we found women's shoes in the closet, but no other clothing of the female variety. The place was a total bachelor pad, though. I can't imagine that a woman lives in that house full-time. No personal touches. Not even a throw pillow or a framed family photo.

Janice did some research. Derek Anderson works for a pharmaceutical company based in the Bay Area. Not a sales rep but a vice president. We think he's here temporarily, probably trying to score some large-scale deals with the Honolulu medical providers.

So, when I pull out my phone and search for the missing woman story, I'm not surprised to learn that Lani Lum is a director at one of our largest medical facilities here in the islands. I'm on my lunch break, over at the park next to the resort, trying to make sense of this. Trying to tell myself that I have no obligation to report that I saw her on property, meeting with Derek Anderson a few days before she went missing.

Her company must have a record of her lunch with Derek Anderson, since it seems to have been a business meeting. Lots of people saw her with him, even if Leo didn't seem to recognize her face. And of course, now that we broke into the guy's house...

But we didn't take anything.

Nobody would put two and two together, if I did tell the cops I saw her.

Staring down at my phone, I see the words that nibble on my innards:

If anyone has any information, please contact...

Taking a deep breath, I stand up, shove my phone in my pocket, and stroll back in the direction of the valet stand.

I'm telling nobody that Lani Lum is the woman I saw with Derek Anderson.

Not even Janice.

Especially Janice, who has a big mouth and a penchant for drama.

Definitely not Tina.

Because there's no serial killer. It's only been a few days since Lani Lum went missing. She's probably fine. The runaway bride's fiancé was brought in for questioning. I have no obligation to this Lum woman.

She's not my problem.

This isn't on me.

Right?

But all I can see in my mind's eye are those pretty-boy hands wrapped around her slender, graceful neck. And Lani Lum, gasping for air.

EIGHT

JOHNNY

"I don't want to move," Janice proclaims.

"What's changed in the last few days?" I ask.

"I'll miss my friends," she says from her stove, as she whips up a stir-fry for dinner. The pungent smells make my mouth water. She's a good cook, and she spoils me in the kitchen, I'll give her that, even if she is hard to read in terms of our relationship.

But her answer surprises me. Janice isn't the type to go out with the girls, at least not that I know of. But then, we don't see each other every night. She's an enigma, and I hate to admit it, but that's part of the attraction. I've always felt a little unsure about her feelings for me, which keeps me on my toes. Not a good foundation for a marriage. I know this.

Not like Linda Chun, my high school girlfriend. Linda was what you'd call marriage material. My mother adored her, and the feeling was mutual. After my dad split and my mom got sick, Linda helped me take care of her. I was an only child, so it fell on me. After my mom's first deployment, when it all fell on my dad and my tutu to take care of me, I guess they figured one kid was enough. It gave my mother comfort in her last days, knowing that I had someone in my life. Someone like my mother. A caregiver.

Except my mom had an edge to her, like Janice. A woman in the military can't be too passive. She also had an abusive father and a mother who didn't protect herself or her kids, which is why she enlisted to begin with, and why I don't have a relationship with anyone from her side of the family. I guess that's the part of Mom I see in Janice. Linda had no spunk.

So, when my mom passed, I dumped Linda.

Why?

I can't tell you.

Maybe she reminded me too much of sad times. All I know is, I needed to run free.

After a year or so living with my tutu, my dad's mom, I scraped up enough money to move to New York. When I heard through the grapevine a few years later that Linda married a California businessman a decade older than her, I have to admit, a little pang of regret stabbed me in the side.

I'm not a sap, though. And while it might seem like Janice has me whipped, she doesn't. Which is why I'm leaving the engagement ring I brought to her place safely tucked away in my pocket. Fuck her, if she wants to play games.

It's a ring I had already, left over from my dad's stash, most of which got liquidated to pay his debts, but not before I lifted a few key pieces for myself. I wasn't about to spend money on a ring for Janice, knowing that she might turn me down.

That should tell you something about the state of this relationship.

I would have bought a ring for Linda.

She would have said yes.

I wonder if Linda Chun is happy now.

I don't protest about Janice's change of heart. Instead, I say, "Okay, but I'm out of the jewelry business."

Janice puts on a pouty face, but she doesn't challenge me. All she says is, "We'll see." Then she comes over and strokes my bicep.

Her mating signal.

But I'm not having it. I'm hungry, plus, I'm a little put off. So, instead of responding like I usually do, I tell her I want to watch the local news. Sometimes I do this, and she thinks it's cute. Kind of old-fashioned. She teases me about it. Tells me I'm an old man waiting to happen, which is fine with me. Being an old man has a certain kind of appeal. The way you can just not give a fuck anymore.

Plopping on her white leather sofa, I say, "Get me a beer, will you, babe? And let's eat here, when it's ready."

"Fine," she says. "In a minute."

The disappearance of Lani Lum is the lead story, which is why I wanted to watch the broadcast. I'm glad I didn't tell Janice that I saw her with our target, and I kind of like that I'm keeping something from her. If she's going to be mysterious, then two can play at that game.

So far, the authorities aren't making a connection to the murdered woman, but the news desk is. First, the screen flashes photos of the two women, side by side. The implications are obvious, but the newscaster stops short of stating it:

"Two women have gone missing. One has been found dead."

Then the report cuts to footage of a news conference that happened earlier in the day. Detective Denise Akana finally takes questions, after giving the public nothing of value, repeating what we already know: one woman is dead, and her fiancé has been brought in for questioning. Lani Lum is still missing. No sign of foul play.

"Is there a connection between the two women?" a reporter asks.

The Royal is a connection, and I wonder if they know that yet.

Detective Akana responds, but there's a slight hesitation in her delivery. "At this time, we have no reason to believe the cases are connected," she says.

An observer shouts out something about the Honolulu Strangler.

"Please," she says. "Don't jump to conclusions. Please be patient and let us do our jobs."

A male reporter yells out, not waiting to be called on. "Can you give us the cause of death for Shayna McCarthy? Is it a homicide?"

"I can't comment on an ongoing investigation," the detective says.

Then she asks again for the public's help, and they're on to a story about a shooting in Kalihi with a suspect in custody. Maybe that's supposed to make us feel safer?

I looked up the Honolulu Strangler case after Tina mentioned it. In that instance, the women didn't look alike, so it doesn't surprise me that it took a while for the cops to make the connection. It was more a crime of opportunity. The killer targeted stranded women. Women waiting for a bus. A car that broke down. Before the era of cell phones, that was a terrifying prospect, being stranded, late at night.

Technically, it's still a cold case, although the FBI is pretty sure they know who did it. The guy was arrested, but they couldn't make it stick. Then he moved off island and the murders stopped. The feds kept tabs on him for decades, but there wasn't enough evidence to convict him.

For a brief moment, I thought, *what if he's back?* I mean, he'd have to be pretty old by now. But I looked it up. That guy they were tracking is dead, and now I wonder why they can't retest the DNA and get closure on that case. They must have his DNA, if they followed him for decades. They're closing cold cases left and right these days with the new technology they have, which makes me suspect that maybe the dead guy wasn't the Honolulu Strangler after all.

There's been a resurgence of interest in the old case. True crime podcasts keep the story alive. Which is good, I suppose. The families need closure, and public interest does serve a purpose beyond morbid curiosity. Pressure and publicity keep the case in the spotlight. But it also makes me think about the possibility of a copycat. So many sickos out there.

If Shayna McCarthy wasn't strangled, that would lessen the chances that it's related to the cold case.

I wish they would tell us the cause of death.

Janice comes in with my Kona Longboard, frosty cold.

She hands it to me. I take a hearty gulp and place it on the pikake flower coaster that sits on her glass coffee table. That's another thing about Janice and me. We have different tastes. She leans toward modern, with clean lines and lots of white. I prefer warmth. A homey feel. Wood. Natural materials. We'd probably argue about whose furniture we'd take with us if we moved.

A few minutes later, she returns with our plates of chicken and veggies over rice. She's mumbling to me as she walks back and forth, but I can't hear what she's saying.

"Did you hear me?" Janice says, as she sits down next to me.

"Did I hear what?"

"The case."

"What case?"

Her brow furrows as she eyes me. "They got cause of death

on Shayna McCarthy. Didn't you just say you wanted to know the cause of death? Or were you talking to yourself again?"

Did I say that out loud?

I don't recall saying that out loud.

Maybe I'm losing it.

"How do you know?" I ask.

"Social media. You know the news broadcasts are always behind these days."

"You can't believe what you read on social media," I tell her. "Remember pizza gate?"

Janice lets out a huff and goes back to her phone without giving me the scoop.

"Well?" I ask.

"Well, what? Are you done mansplaining to me about the veracity of social media? I'm not an idiot, Johnny. I vet my sources."

"What are your *sources* saying on social media?"

"Fuck off, if you're not going to take me seriously." She turns from me and starts eating her chicken plate.

Tickling her, I offer an apology of sorts. "I'm a man. I mansplain. It's what we do. Just, come on, babe. Tell me."

"She died of a drug overdose," Janice reports. "They think it might be insulin, but that hasn't been confirmed."

"Drug overdose, huh? Then it must not be the Honolulu Strangler."

"That case is decades old. The guy is dead. Why would you even go there?"

"Tina mentioned it, so I looked it up. I wondered why—"

"Tina? Again?"

Again?

But then she says, "You know who could have access to insulin?"

"Tina?"

She rolls her eyes and bats me on the arm. "Someone who works in big pharma. Someone who has women's shoes in his closet. Someone like Derek Anderson." Janice stares me down a little too long, and I feel as if she can read my mind.

Images of Lani Lum spin in my head.

Does Janice know something?

Did I perhaps mention out loud that I saw Lani Lum?

Like I forgot to keep that last thought inside my head?

But we're not talking about Lani Lum, I remind myself.

We're talking about Shayna McCarthy.

And just because Derek Anderson has a bunch of pharmaceutical sample cases in his rental, it doesn't mean he's a serial killer. We have no evidence that he even knew the first victim. Yes, the news said she was found clothed but barefoot, but that doesn't mean those were her shoes in his closet. They didn't even say what kind of shoes she was wearing. No insulin vials were in his kits, and that would be one of the easier drugs to get. Janice actually suggested we take the drugs and sell them on the black market. I hope she was joking, because that's crazy talk for sure.

"That's a stretch," I say. "Lots of diabetes in the island. It could be any number of people. But you could leave an anonymous tip, if you really think he's the guy."

"No," she says. "I bet they tap the phones."

"So? We didn't take anything. What does it matter?"

Now, Janice looks like a six-year-old child who ate a pack of chocolate chip cookies right before dinner. I've never seen her look so sheepish. "Don't kill me," she says.

"What, Jan? Tell me you didn't take the dr—"

She holds up a hand. "Cufflinks. I took the diamond cufflinks. Sorry, Johnny. I didn't want to leave empty-handed. Don't worry. He'll probably think he forgot them back in Cali."

"You'd better hope so. If he actually is a serial killer, I'd hate to get on his bad side."

I wish she didn't take the stupid cufflinks, but it's better than taking the drugs.

"If he actually is a serial killer, maybe we could get more evidence and blackmail him. I'm sure he's loaded. He's a Silicon Valley VP."

My jaw drops.

Blackmail him?

Is she losing it?

She whips her head back and cackles. "You should have seen your face, Johnny! That was priceless. I'm not going to blackmail a serial killer," she says. "I'm not that reckless."

"So now we've decided that Derek Anderson is a serial killer?"

Janice shrugs. "I guess we'll see. I'll keep an eye on him."

My girlfriend's not stupid, but she just might be insane.

So, I'll keep an eye on Janice, keeping an eye on Derek Anderson. And for the second time today, I wonder what my old flame Linda Chun is up to these days.

NINE

JOHNNY

Tina hands me a key card encased in a smooth black leather holder.

Turning to my right, I see him.

Tesla Guy.

But he doesn't see me. I know I said I'd keep an eye out for him, but this feels eerie, almost as if he's here, testing me. Like he knows I'm on to him. Like he knows I was in his house poking through his stuff.

"What's wrong, Johnny?" Tina says.

I've been staring into space too long. Shaking my head, I say, "I think I forgot to turn the a/c off at home."

Then I head off with a light jog to fetch his car.

Perspiration dampens my palms as they wrap around his key card. My stomach is in knots by the time I reach the garage. When I'm nervous, I sweat bullets. Wiping my hands on my pants before I grab the steering wheel, I will myself to calm down.

He's not a serial killer. He's just a rich asshole who I happen to know is a semi-regular here. There's no way he knows I was in his house. Taking a deep breath, I start up his car and drive it over to the curb in front of the valet desk.

My pulse quickens when I see him talking to Tina.

Tina, who looks like the missing women.

I think about the fact that Tina has a nine-millimeter in her home, and I wonder if she has the balls to use it. They seem familiar, almost like he's chatting her up. He's not usually too friendly. That time at lunch, he didn't even wait for Lani Lum to get her car back from Leo. Maybe he's in a better mood today. Or maybe the aloha spirit is rubbing off on him. Or maybe he's found his next victim.

Stop the crazy.

Pulling up to the curb, I puff up my chest, exit the vehicle, and look him square in the eye. When I hand him the key card, he slaps a five in my hand and holds my gaze without flinching. His eyes are dark and haunting, and I wonder if they are the last thing Shayna McCarthy saw before she took her final breath.

Without a thank you, he drives off.

Sinking my shoulders, I let out a sigh of relief, grab another set of keys, and hop in the next car that needs to be parked, although I'm dying to find out what he and Tina were talking about. But when I return, Tina's gone. Mandy, one of the front desk workers, is covering for her. We're swamped today, and we're understaffed, so I'm not getting answers any time soon. Instead, I zone out and do my job for a hot, steamy hour, somewhat grateful for the distraction.

ON MY LUNCH BREAK, I pull out my phone, and I'm almost embarrassed to admit what I do next. I start looking on social media for my old girlfriend Linda Chun. I don't know why she's on my mind so much these days. Perhaps it's because I was thinking about popping the question to Janice, and then I started to get cold feet. I suppose it's only natural that I'd reflect on my last serious relationship, and that was with Linda.

Linda's single now?

According to her social media status, she is.

But she lives in San Diego.

I'm sure I heard she got married, back when I was in LA, and my stomach flutters a little when I think about the fact that she's available.

But why wouldn't it say divorced on her social media page?

Maybe I heard she was engaged, not married?

I don't remember. I saw it on a friend of a friend's feed years ago, and at that time, I was playing the field, and I wasn't going to get too worked up about an old flame getting married. Lots of hot women in LA. And at that point, I wanted someone more exciting than Linda, who had been pretty tame and predictable, from my recollection.

It's not like I'm bored with Janice or that I'm itching to put myself out there again. But one of the incentives for staying in a relationship and working on it is you've got time in, and if you start from scratch, you never know what kind of crazy you might get. At least with Janice, I know where the bodies are buried, even if she is a little unhinged sometimes.

But with Linda, it wouldn't be like starting over. I already know her. Sure, she seemed a little dull to me when I was young, but right now, that could be exactly what I need. At least she won't land me in prison, or get me tortured by a serial killer.

So, I do some more digging to try and find out more about my now-single ex-girlfriend. Searching up her name, a bunch of articles appear, almost too quickly. Skimming a few headlines, I get the gist and... holy crap.

She's a widow?

Damn. That makes me feel old, and I'm not that old. Neither is she. Early thirties is not old. But she married an older guy with a lot of money. He died in a boating accident. No kids, according to the article.

"Hey!" Leo's voice jolts me back to the present.

I quick turn over the phone and slip it in my back pants pocket.

Leo chuckles. "What? You got a porno there, Johnny Boy?"

"Shut up," I say.

"I hate this shift," he says, and he takes a seat next to me on the bench.

This is a nice spot to hang out during our break. It's to the side of the property, in front of a small beach park. There's not much beach, but it's peaceful and shaded with coconut palms, tall ones that sway in the breeze. I love looking at palm trees. I find it relaxing. If I move, I'd miss the palm trees. Maybe I should think about Florida.

The water's calm today, with a hint of white foam gracing the turquoise water as gentle waves lap the shore. Too bad I'm sweating my balls off, even though it's overcast. It's late May, and it's already too hot to sit here most days. Then I have to take my break in the air-conditioned corners of the resort that are open to staff. Ones with no view.

Leo likes to work mornings, but today he's starting after lunch, in the heat of the day. He's a little early. We have great weather here, it's true, but not if you're out in the sun all day. It's brutal here, and even with the trades we get most days, it can be super taxing on the body. He's old to still be doing this job, but I guess he can't retire. His wife has some health issues, and we have great insurance.

"You ever think about leaving this place?" I ask, turning to look at him.

"I can't retire yet. Got responsibilities," he says. Leo looks a little haggard, I notice. More than usual. The lines on his weathered face seem more pronounced; his sagging jawline a little more flaccid, like he's dropped some weight.

"No, not the job. The islands," I say.

Leo shakes his head. "Me? No. I'm dug in. Got my mom to take care of. My wife. We've got Mom's house now, pretty much paid for. No reason to go. Why? You thinking about it?"

Needing to confide in someone, I take a deep breath and feel my shoulders sink at the possibility of unburdening myself to someone besides Janice. "Yeah. It's a struggle here. I talked to Janice about Vegas or Reno and she seemed interested, but then she changed her mind."

"Janice? You serious about that one?" Leo's tone of voice conveys his opinion about this prospect.

Shrugging, I say, "I guess? It's about time I settle down. Why?"

Leo has only met Janice a few times. At the company Christmas parties, and once at their twentieth wedding anniversary celebration, and she seemed to be on her best behavior, so this surprises me.

My coworker shakes his head. "It's not my place. Forget it."

"I don't mind, Leo. Truthfully, I'm having second thoughts about the relationship. I'd like a fresh opinion, from someone who's gone the distance."

Hesitating for a moment, he continues. "I don't like it when she shows up here, checking up on you."

My brow furrows. "Checking up on me? What are you talking about?"

Leo hesitates, then continues. "She comes here sometimes. Looking for you. Like last week, for example. I remember, because it was the day you parked the Roadster, and it seemed like you were sitting in the car, talking on the phone with her.

But then I'd seen her on property about twenty minutes before, so it confused me."

"Oh yeah," I say, trying to think on my feet. She had to bring me some paperwork."

"What kind of paperwork?" Leo asks.

"Um, some stuff for my condo. Not important." Glancing at my watch, I add, "Shit. I need to get going."

Leo smirks, and something tells me he's even more suspicious now than he was before. Why did I cover for Janice? It's better that he thinks she's a stalker. But this news surprises me. I thought Janice and I were past that. She did it a few times when we first got together, popped in on me at work. Not recently, though. At least not that I know of.

"Sure. I'll be over in thirty. Be careful there, Johnny Boy," he says.

Careful about what?

When I approach the valet station, I'm shocked to see Tina standing to the side of the desk, talking to a cop. My first thought is that her ex is back. That he's come after her again.

Running up to her, I place a hand on her arm and ask, "Are you okay?"

She shoots me a look that makes me realize I've crossed some imaginary boundary. That my concern for her is ill-timed and inappropriate.

"Sir?" the officer says. "This is a private conversation."

He's a young pup, around early twenties. Smaller guy with rounded shoulders and body language that screams of insecurity. Still, my stomach sinks as my mind flashes to an image of me rifling through Derek Anderson's file. Then I notice that the general manager is behind the desk, doing Tina's job.

First Mandy filling in for Tina, and now this?

What on earth is happening?

Whatever it is, the cars are backed up like crazy.

"Johnny!" my GM says. "Get these cars out of here, will you?"

He tosses me a key, and I hop to it. Instead of answers, I only have more questions. Two cop cars sit in our staging area, but they're not pulled all the way in, so I have to maneuver around them. This only adds to the congestion.

I get the first car through the narrow space when I see Leo running over. They must have called him in to start early. After twenty minutes or so, we get the log jam cleared, and I finally have a chance to find out what happened.

"They found that missing woman," Leo says. "The one Tina showed us on her phone the other day."

From the look on his face and the two cop cars, I'm guessing it's not great news for Lani Lum. "What happened?"

"She's dead," Leo says, with almost no emotion behind his delivery.

This sends a chill up my spine, although it's hot as hell.

Lani Lum is dead?

"What does that have to do with the Royal?" I ask.

Leo shrugs, the kind of shrug that indicates a lack of interest in the topic rather than bewilderment. "I don't know. Someone found her body at Paiko Lagoon. I guess she was here for lunch last week, right before she disappeared. Same like that runaway bride. They want to interview anyone who came in contact with her. She met with that Tesla guy over lunch."

"What Tesla guy?"

Of course, I know who he means, but I don't want to appear obsessed with him. Paiko Lagoon is near his house, too, and I fight to suppress a reaction.

"The one with the Roadster who got under your skin. Remember? You parked his car. You were sitting in it, talking on the phone, dope." Leo bats me on the arm. "The day Janice was here?"

"Oh, right," I say.

Did I tell Leo I didn't like the guy?

I've barely had time to process the idea of Janice being here that day, and now I've got a dead woman who was also seen at our hotel. I have to admit, if this one also died of an insulin overdose, a pharmaceutical executive might look a little suspicious. Maybe Janice is on to something.

But how would Derek Anderson be connected to the other woman?

The runaway bride?

"You got her car," I say. "Don't they want to talk to you?"

Leo narrows his eyes at me. "How do you know I got her car?"

"Didn't you?" I ask.

"It was busy. I don't remember getting her car."

"You did. I saw you drop it at the curb and hand her the key."

Leo's head tilts to the side. "How do you know it was the dead woman?"

"What do you mean?" I ask.

Then my insides seize up, and my vision starts to narrow.

A shot of adrenaline courses through my veins, making my pulse pound as I realize how badly I screwed up.

Leo confirms what I've already deduced. "I mean, I don't remember seeing her. We all looked at Tina's photo of her, and you didn't *say* you remembered seeing her here. So how do you know, all of a sudden, that I got her car?"

Rivulets of sweat run down the side of my face. I wipe them away as I struggle to form a response. Puddles form under my armpits, despite being slathered in heavy-duty antiperspirant. I can only hope they don't soak through my shirt and vest.

"I guess it clicked," I say.

"Sure, Johnny. It doesn't have anything to do with what you were doing, sitting in that Roadster, now does it?"

"I was talking on my cell, to Janice."

"Janice. Who was here, giving you some paperwork."

"Right," I say.

"You'd better get your story straight, Johnny Boy. They don't fuck around with murder."

SITTING in the open-air lobby with the cop who seems to be in charge, I manage to calm myself down and give what I think is a reasonable explanation for why I noticed Lani Lum that day.

"The guy was kind of a prick," I say to Officer Yoshimura. "I felt sorry for her. Nice local girl like that. I thought, *what's she doing with a guy like him?* He didn't even wait for her to get her car."

"The guy she had lunch with?" Yoshimura asks. This cop is an older guy, around Leo's age. I'm sure he's heard it all. He seems pretty local, so I'm trying to connect with him on that level.

"Yeah," I say. "The guy who drove the Tesla Roadster."

"How was he a prick?" Yoshimura asks.

"You know, not from here. Rude. He's been here before, so I remembered him. Never even says thanks when I give him his car. You know the type."

The officer gives me a hard stare. "No. I do not know the type. So. You fancied this Lani Lum? Is that what I'm hearing? Thought she could do better?"

"No! It's not like that. I have a girlfriend. Janice Nunes. Ask Leo. She was here that day."

"I'm asking you. Did you find Lani Lum attractive?"

I shrug. "She's okay, I guess. She's not really my type."

"Why not?"

"Too tall for me. I'm on the shorter side, as you may have noticed."

"Do tall women piss you off?" he asks.

"What? No. Do I need a lawyer?"

"I don't know. Do you?"

Then he asks me a question that has no good answer. He asks why I didn't recognize her the day Leo and Tina and I were looking at her photo. I give him the only answer I can think of that makes any sense at all, with a partial truth embedded in it, which I hope will help me sell it.

"I didn't look very closely at Tina's phone, to tell you the truth. There was a glare on the screen, and I thought Tina was being hysterical. She's kind of obsessed with serial killers. Even after that first woman was found, which we all thought was the fiancé, she was going on and on about some case from the eighties. The Honolulu Strangler. How the cops didn't put two and two together. That it could be another serial killer. I was kind of humoring her. Pretending to listen."

Officer Yoshimura's got a good poker face, and I can't tell if he's buying it. "But all of a sudden, you remember seeing Lani Lum here that day. How is that?"

"It wasn't all of a sudden. I saw her photo on the news later that night," I say. "And then it clicked."

"Clicked?"

"Yeah. It clicked. They had more photos on the news, and one of them jogged my memory."

"Yet you didn't call in a tip."

"I... ah, I meant to. But my girlfriend and me. We were kind of in the middle of something. I got distracted. Sorry."

"Girlfriend problems?" he says.

I shrug. "Just the normal stuff."

"So maybe you wanted to trade up? Get Lani Lum away from the prick? And maybe she turned you down?"

"It's not like that," I say. "Are we done here? I need to get back to work."

He stares at me a good long time and says, "Go. But don't go far."

ELEVEN

JOHNNY

The lunch rush is over, and now it's Tina's turn to have a go at me. We're hanging by the valet desk, trying to make sense of it all. She tells me she found out about Lani Lum's murder from "Derek," who she's now apparently on a first name basis with. The cops asked him to meet with them here, so he could take them through the victim's movements that day.

She explains the situation to me. "Leo doesn't remember getting her car, but I told the cops that he did. I remembered the car, but not her, because Derek handed me both tickets. He said she went to the ladies' room. I gave Leo the ticket after you said you'd grab the Roadster."

Then she asks me why I didn't recognize Lani Lum when she showed me the photo.

"Dementia runs in my family," I say. "Maybe with me, it comes and goes."

"This is serious, Johnny," she says. "A woman was murdered. The cops asked me about it. About if you looked hard at the photo. I guess Leo told them he thought it was odd that you told him he got her car, but you didn't remember seeing her when I showed you guys the photo. I told the cop I wasn't sure, but that was kind of a lie."

"I did look at your phone, but there was a glare on the screen. You never need to lie for me. I have nothing to hide."

She seems to accept my explanation, so I change the subject, hoping to leave it at that.

"Tina," I say. "Has Janice been here on property lately? Looking for me?"

"Your girlfriend, Janice?"

"Yeah. Do you know another Janice?"

She shoots me a sideways glance.

"Sorry," I offer. "Didn't mean to be such a wise ass. I'm a little stressed."

"We're all stressed, Johnny. It's not an excuse to be rude. And no, I haven't seen Janice around. Why?"

"It's just, Leo said Janice comes here looking for me sometimes."

Tina's eyes widen. "Looking for you? That doesn't sound good. Take it from me."

That's right. Tina's husband was a violent stalker. Maybe this is hard for her to talk about. Pressing on, I ask, "But you haven't seen her around?"

Tina shakes her head no. "But I've only met her in passing. I'm not sure I would even notice her, and I'm kind of surprised that Leo would. She gave me a vibe at the last Christmas party, not a good one."

"What kind of vibe?"

"A 'stay away from my man' vibe."

This surprises me. When we first got together, Janice could get a little jealous. She'd call me on it if I looked too hard at another woman when we were out. That sort of thing. But she had a point. Sometimes my eyes lingered a little too long on an ample butt as it wiggled away, or a killer rack, if it was right in my face. It didn't mean anything. Men are visual. But it was a bad habit, and I trained myself to stop. I thought we were past it, but maybe not.

Come to think of it, Janice made a comment about Tina the other day, didn't she?

Tina again?

Something like that.

"Are you two serious?" Tina asks.

"Define serious. We're exclusive. We don't live together. We don't talk much about the future."

Tina shrugs. "Well, if I were you, I'd think twice about being serious about a woman who shows up at your work, checking up on you."

"You do have a point."

But the thing is, I only have Leo's word for it that Janice does this. He has no reason to lie that I can think of, but then you never know. I have a feeling he suspects something about my little side hustle. But how would that factor into gaslighting me about Janice? Maybe he wants me to dump her and partner up with him? Maybe he plans to blackmail me?

Also, Tina has a point. Leo hasn't met Janice many times, but he says he saw her here. Yet he seemed oblivious to the fact that Lani Lum was here, and she's an attractive woman, like Janice. So how come he didn't notice Lani Lum?

Maybe he did.

Maybe Leo is lying.

For now, I leave it. I'll try to find a way to figure out if Janice was here that day. Maybe I can check the GPS on her car. I'm so glad I didn't ask her to marry me. I realize now that Janice is a bit of a closed book. She never tells me what's going on in her head, and that's not a healthy basis for a relationship.

Moving away from Honolulu is something I want to do for myself. And if she doesn't want to come with me, then I'll go alone. Plus, I don't like the fact that we agreed to move and then she changed her mind. What if we plan a wedding and she does an about-face, like Shayna McCarthy did? That had to be totally humiliating for her guy.

I'll crunch the numbers. See what my condo is worth. I need a fresh start, that's for sure. And maybe it's better if I go it alone. And one thing is for sure. If we decide to go our separate ways, I have to get her to break up with me. If I dump her, she's liable to get vengeful. She knows too much.

And since I live alone, she could be my only alibi, in case the cops try to make something of this Lani Lum murder and my facial recognition faux pas. The evening of the day Lani Lum was seen here, I stayed at Janice's place. My car is old and it doesn't have GPS. Maybe my phone does, though. I'll check, as soon as I get home.

If only I knew when Lani Lum was abducted.

Or when she was murdered.

"Johnny?" Tina says.

I've been staring into space too long.

"Yeah?"

"That day Lani Lum was here. Why did you cut the line to go get the Roadster?"

My heart is immediately in my throat, reverberating into my eardrums as they throb and pulsate. It wasn't lost on Tina that I wanted to get back to the car. My ticker is pounding so hard, it feels like I'm having a heart attack, but I'm not. I get like this sometimes, like when people start to think I'm a killer. I fight to keep this from exploding into a full-blown panic attack.

Breathe.

The pools of sweat that stayed safely nestled behind the wall of fabric now seep through to the outside. I'm off in twenty minutes. I need to make it through the rest of my shift, and then I can regroup.

Right about now, I'm thinking my best option might be to get a lawyer and come clean about all of it. Tell Janice I'll leave her out of it. Tesla Guy was a wiseass. I went to steal his watch. All I got were some stupid cufflinks. Now I think he might be a serial killer. I'll make a deal. They'll match those shoes to the missing women. I'll be a hero.

Yeah, right.

After way too long of a pause, I respond, "It's a fun car to drive."

Then I shrug at her.

Tina gives me a head nod, and we leave it at that.

What I said is true, and I'm more than a little impressed with myself for pulling that out of my ass. Then I excuse myself for a bathroom break as the polyester fabric of my vest turns a darker shade of blue, hoping that I can keep all the balls I'm juggling up in the air, but feeling like they're about to come tumbling down around me.

TWELVE
JOHNNY

There are certain unknowns I'll have to live with for the time being. I don't know who killed the two women. I don't know if Derek Anderson is a serial killer or just your garden-variety jackass. I don't know if the police think I had something to do with it.

But there is one unknown I can do something about. I've thought this through, and I don't see a real downside to coming out and asking her.

After a very stressful day, we're strolling around Ala Moana Center, a large, open-air mall Janice loves, window shopping at upscale establishments on our way to Macy's to get her some new sheets. Then we were planning to catch happy hour at Morton's. She likes to sit at the bar and have drinks and pupus. The crab cakes there are "to die for," according to my girl, and thinking about them, I realize I'm hungry. I could wait until we're at the bar to ask her, but it's a lively spot and we might get distracted, so I take a deep breath and get it over with.

"Hey, Jan. Leo said he saw you at the Royal, the day I

landed on Anderson as our next target. Was he seeing things, or were you there?"

She stops and turns to me, right in front of Neiman Marcus. Her brow furrows and her mouth hangs open as she leans her head to the side, eyeing me with a look I can't quite place. She's not mad. Or indignant, which is what I expected.

She looks... worried?

The only other time I've seen this look on my girlfriend's face is when her mother nearly collapsed at a potluck New Year's Eve party a few years back, and we had to rush her to the ER. I remember because I had to dodge the fireworks fodder. I thought an aerial might hit the gas tank and cause the car to explode into a ball of fire. I vowed never to go out on New Year's again.

Still, she hasn't spoken yet. But when she does, it comes out almost as a whisper. "Johnny? Are you okay?"

Now it's my turn to look puzzled. "What do you mean?"

"I mean, we talked about this! That same night. I told you I met a client at the Royal for coffee. And then I looked for you, but we missed each other. I even sent you a text while I was there, but you didn't answer. Remember?"

But I don't remember.

Janice sends me a lot of texts.

She tells me a lot of things, and sometimes I don't listen.

Sure, it's possible she did both of those things. I don't want to call her out on it or check my text messages with her standing right in front of me, so for now, I make light of it.

"Oh, I must not have heard you. Maybe I need to get my hearing checked."

Shaking her head, she accepts my retort, and we continue on our mission.

It's possible my hearing is impaired. Too much gaming. Deafening concerts at Aloha Stadium. It's also possible she's bullshitting me. But there's another possibility I may need to consider, and I don't like it at all.

It's possible that I need to cut back on the weed.

No, not cut back.

Cut out.

This isn't the first time my memory has failed me. And that night, I was high. That probably contributes to my habit of talking to myself. It screws up my perceptions. If I'm going to try to figure out what the hell is going on, I need to have a clear head. As much as I hate to admit it, the stuff fucks with my head. The weed is so much stronger now than it used to be. I've tried to wean myself with CBD gummies, but it's not the same.

I'll admit it. I like the high.

Who am I kidding?

I love the high.

But clearly, it doesn't love me. I need to stop. It's not like I do it every single day. In fact, today is Monday, and I haven't imbibed since Saturday night. Maybe it'll be fine. I've been wanting to quit for a while now, and this is as good a reason as any. Besides, if they do pin a murder on me, it'll be one less thing I'll miss in prison.

OUR EVENING WENT WELL, all things considered. Janice scored some high-thread-count Egyptian cotton sheets and got a great discount; she was quite pleased with herself. I must admit, they are much more comfortable than any sheets I've tried, short of the ones we use at the Royal. She was so excited when we got home that she washed and dried them and made us have sex on the sofa so they would remain pristine. I think she loves the sheets more than she loves me.

Morton's was fun. We chatted with the couple next to us,

empty nesters looking to downsize, so Janice may have even picked up a new client. I only had one drink because I was the designated driver. And no bedtime gummy, as I've decided to go cold turkey.

That's why I'm up, flat on my back staring at the ceiling at two in the morning, listening to Janice and her slight wheezing. This might be tougher than I thought to kick the habit. Insomnia was one of the reasons I started with the stuff to begin with.

But my head is pretty clear, so there's that. I did go back to the string of texts she sent me that day. It's hard to tell when she said what, because my phone doesn't always give a precise time, especially if there's a cascade of messages on my phone screen, like there were on that day. And yes, there are a few texts that seem to suggest she was looking for me, but nothing that explicitly states she's at the Royal.

The closest is:

Where are you? I wanted to say hi.

It would be nice if I could trust Leo and Janice. For now, I decide that I can.

And if Leo and Janice are both telling the truth, then my biggest problem is that I screwed up about seeing Lani Lum. I think my explanation will hold for now about the glare on the phone screen. There's nothing tying me to Shayna McCarthy at all, besides the fact that she was at the Royal. I have no way to get insulin, if that truly is the drug that killed her. That hasn't been confirmed yet.

The trouble is, I'm a bad liar. Sweating is my tell, and if it ever comes to the point where I'm sitting under those bright lights with the bad cop badgering me hour after hour, they'll know in a heartbeat that I was lying. That I studied Lani Lum's face that day. And I'll need to give them a reason that doesn't make me look like a serial killer.

Still, I didn't murder her. All I did was break into a house. Now I want to search up the maximum penalty for burglary, but I don't dare move a muscle. Janice is a light sleeper, and I don't want to wake her. I kind of like the quiet, being alone with my thoughts, which are getting sharper by the minute.

The idea of making a deal slips back into my mind, along with myriad other random thoughts that race through my unmedicated brain. Helping the cops catch a serial killer. Being a hero. That would be something, wouldn't it? He's probably not a murderer, though. But it is weird that the guy has women's shoes in his closet but no other women's clothing.

They say killers like to take trophies.

Were those his trophies?

Shoes would make good trophies.

Maybe he has a shoe fetish.

I wish we had taken a photo of those shoes.

If he thinks they're on to him, he'll get rid of the evidence.

I need proof if I'm going to the cops.

And then another thought pops into my head.

It's kind of risky, but it excites me.

I could go back to his bedroom and get a photo of the shoes.

Or I could take a gummy and get some sleep.

JOHNNY

Rather than doing something rash, I decide to pay a visit to my second cousin once removed, which makes him my dad's cousin and more the age of an uncle. But technically, that's what he is. My cousin, who is also a retired HPD officer. To me, he's Uncle Mel.

I've avoided him ever since Janice and I started our little side business because, as I said, I'm a bad liar. He's asked me to get together a few times, but I've never taken him up on it. He was so disappointed in my dad, and I'd hate to do that to him again.

I wonder, if I hadn't gotten involved with Janice, would I have gone down this path? I want to think not, but I also need to take responsibility for my actions. The skeletons in my closet are mine to own.

We're meeting at the Honu Club, Mel's favorite spot. I have two days off, and I plan to make the most of them. He's asked me to join the organization a few times, but I think he's given up on me. Since I live within walking distance of the establishment, it would make sense for me. It's right on the ocean with a killer view, but it's more his speed than mine. Maybe if I had kids, I'd join for the pool. But it's not exactly crawling with singles my age. From the few times I've been here, it seems to go from young families to people Mel's age, with not much in between.

Uncle Mel looks quite at home here, though. Bellied up to the bar at two in the afternoon, he's drinking a Corona with his cronies. This is a problem for me. I need to talk to him alone.

His face lights up as I approach, and he springs up from his perch at the bar.

"Hey! Johnny!" Mel slaps me on the back, then introduces me to his bar buddies as his nephew, Johnny Silva. He stops short of hugging me. Instead, he grips my arm and says, "It's great to see you, son."

This nearly knocks the wind out of me. The emotional punch I feel, hearing those words after so long. I'd always planned to reach out to my father someday, after I cooled off. I was angry with him. And then he crashed into a tree on a drunken bender, and it was too late.

Mel's pretty much the only family I have left, and the thought of doing something to make him proud. Being a hero. Putting a serial killer behind bars. Well, it almost takes my breath away. But disappointing him is far more likely, and that possibility twists my stomach into knots.

I'm not sure how much I can tell him, especially in front of a crowd. I'm not sure I can tell him anything at all. Maybe this was a mistake.

"Let's get a table," he says to me. "What'll you have?" he says.

"A beer's good. Corona."

The bartender hears us. It's not too crowded, and soon, a cold one is in my hand and we're making our way to a table out near the water. We're so close to the shoreline, it's like being on a cruise. This place would never get built with the setbacks they have now. When the king tide comes in, seawater can sometimes splash over the retaining wall and onto the patrons.

Today, though, it's spectacular—an aqua sea with small white caps spilling over the glassy surface. Beyond the reef, a few surfers vie for the occasional wave.

"So, to what do I owe the pleasure?" Mel says.

I shrug. "Can't a guy want to see his uncle for no reason?"

Mel smirks. "I was your age once. So, no, I don't think my single thirty-something nephew is here for no reason. But whatever it is, I'm happy you're here."

"Mel. I'm sorry. I meant to—"

He holds up a hand. "No. Look, it's not like that with me. It's life. When I was young, I did what I wanted to do. I'm happy if you're happy, but I'm here if you need me. We're family. That's how it works."

Taking a sip of my beer, I nod as I decide how to start.

"So," he says. "What's wrong?"

"You watch the news," I say.

"Yeah. And I think it's safe to assume you're not a murderer. So why are they looking at you? Is that what you want to know?"

My stomach sinks. "They're looking at me? For real?"

"They're looking at anyone and everyone who might have had a connection to the two women, and you're a connection. That's about all I know. My contacts know we're related, so my access is a little limited."

"Is it because of my dad?"

"Your dad wasn't a serial killer."

"Neither am I. I mean, is there something specific about me? Do I need an attorney?"

"I don't know. Do you?"

This isn't going the way I envisioned it, and the deluge is

about to begin. I feel the sweat seeping from my pores, which I swear must be the size of golf balls about now. It won't be long until I'm drenched.

"I had nothing to do with those women and what happened to them. That's the god's honest truth."

"Well, I would hope not. But that's not what we're talking about. I'm asking if you have something to hide. Something more along the lines of what runs in your family. And don't answer me on that. I'm just saying. Hypothetically speaking. That would make you more... vulnerable."

I let my shoulders sink. My pores tighten a little, the sweat narrowing to more of a trickle than a flow. Because now, I don't have to lie, but I need to choose my words carefully.

Mel folds his arms, leaning back in his chair, now looking more like a cop and less like an uncle. "So, is that why you want to see me? To find out what they have on you?"

My eyes widen. "No! See, there's this guy at the resort. I have a bad feeling about him, and I don't know what to do about it. That's why I wanted to talk to you."

"Employee?"

"No. A patron. Newly transplanted. Sort of becoming a regular at the Royal. I think it's odd that the murders started recently, around the time he started to frequent our place. He had lunch with Lani Lum, right before she went missing."

"Oh yeah. The cops know about that guy. What do you know that they don't know?"

And now I have to stop short of telling him the rest. If he knows we broke into Derek Anderson's house and saw women's shoes and a slew of pharmaceutical samples, Mel either has to turn me in, or he becomes my accomplice. I can't put him in that position. If I'm going all the way on this, I need to keep Uncle Mel out of it.

"It's just a feeling. You know that cold case? The Honolulu Strangler?"

"Yeah," he says. "What about it?"

"Well, we did some digging. They thought it might have been related to the Green River Killer in Seattle, right? I mean, it wasn't, but for a while, they thought so."

"Who's we?"

"Me and Janice. My girl. She's into true crime."

"They caught the Green River Killer. He had nothing to do with our murders."

"No. that's not what I'm implying. It's an analogy, Uncle Mel. What if the cops look at unsolved murders or disappearances in the Bay Area, where Derek Anderson is from? Maybe if they stopped when he left and started when he got here. Maybe they could get a warrant? Search his house?"

"It's hard to get a warrant based only on circumstantial evidence. But you certainly seem to know a lot about this Anderson guy, I'll give you that."

"Yeah. Like I said, Janice is into the story. And so is this girl at work. Tina. She's kind of obsessed with serial killers. I guess I got the bug from them."

"You know that sometimes killers like to insert themselves into investigations," Mel says.

"That's not what this is!"

"I know that. But that's how it might look."

"So, if I have a bad feeling about this guy, what do I do?"

"You do nothing. Let the cops do their jobs. It's not that easy to pin a murder on an innocent person these days. Juries expect solid evidence. DNA. If you had nothing to do with those women's deaths, then you don't need to worry about that. But the more you go poking around in Derek Anderson's life, the guiltier you'll look."

"Hypothetically speaking, what if a person did know something the cops didn't know, but they want to keep their name out of it?"

"Hypothetically speaking, they could call in an anonymous tip."

"They don't trace those things?"

"I don't like where this is going. Let's try another hypothetical. How's that?"

"Sure," I say.

"Let's say a guy wasn't a murderer, but there's something he's done that can get him in some trouble, with the cops poking around. He needs to get ahead of it. Protect himself. Unburden himself. Tell someone what he knows that he can't tell the cops. There are two people he could go to for guidance, and neither of them is his retired cop uncle. Do we understand each other?"

I shrug. "He could go to an attorney?"

"Bingo."

"Who's the second person?"

Mel shrugs. "If he's thinking long term, he could go to his priest."

FOURTEEN
JOHNNY

"Hey," Janice says, sneaking up on me.

Slamming my phone down, I bark at her. "What the hell?"

She's in front of me now, but she could have seen my phone screen. With her mouth half open, my girl looks a little taken aback. "What is wrong with you today?" she says. "And what's with that look on your face?"

"Nothing," I tell her. "There's no look on my face. That's just my face."

Usually, she'd be pissed at me for snapping at her, but now, she looks almost... frightened. I'm irritable, which they say is one of the withdrawal symptoms. I need to watch it. I bit off Leo's head at work yesterday, too.

"Sorry, babe," I say. "You startled me."

"Yeah, right," she says.

She turns from me and walks out of her living room. We're at her place again. I'm reeling from what I saw on my phone. That wasn't lost on Janice, who could have possibly seen my phone screen, but I doubt she'd have been able to make much sense of it.

At least I hope she couldn't.

Because Linda Chun sent me a friend request.

I must have somehow tweaked the algorithm when I poked around on her page. Once I apologize to Janice, I'll have to think of something to tell her that explains the look on my face. There's no message attached to Linda's friend request, and I suppose the smart thing to do is ignore it. For now, that's what I do.

After a bit, Janice comes back into the living room and says, "We need to talk."

Probably the four worst words a guy can hear coming out of a woman's mouth. Right up there with, "I poisoned your dinner," but at least in the latter case, you could run out the door and get your stomach pumped. Right now, I'm a captive.

"Look, Jan. I'm sorry. I'm on edge. You know I'm trying to kick the weed. Today is day three. After that, I should be back to normal."

"It's not only that," she says. "I think we both know that things haven't felt right lately. Is there anything you want to tell me?"

"Tell you? No. Why? Does this have something to do with me wanting to retire our little venture? Or move away from Honolulu?"

She takes a deep breath and slowly blows it out through a pair of pursed lips. So kissable they are, even under these circumstances. Then she sits next to me and places a hand on mine, which seems serious. Her eyes look heavy, filled with something other than anger. She almost seems hurt, which doesn't make much sense when she says, "I think maybe we need to take a break."

My eyes pop open. "A break? Why?"

I know I said I needed to try and get Janice to break up

with me, but this is coming out of nowhere, and I can't help but sense there's more to this.

Does she somehow know that I've been poking around Linda's social media?

Has she seen my search history?

Looked at my page?

She knows Linda's name. We went through a rundown of past relationships about a month after we started dating. I talked about Linda more in the context of my mom and how she helped me get through it. Maybe Linda showed up on her social media feed, too. I think that's how those apps work. They ping on friends of friends. And if she has, that is not good, especially with what she has on me. I don't need her vengeful and jealous. Who knows what she might do?

That's the trouble with break-ups. When you're intimate with a woman, you let your guard down. Allow yourself to be vulnerable. And the thought of someone out there, armed with all that information about you? It's a frightening prospect, even under normal circumstances. Maybe they'll spill your little secrets. Let people know your innermost thoughts, hopes, dreams, and secret fears.

But in this case, it's way worse than that. Because Janice has stuff on me that could land me in prison. If she wanted to screw with me, she could. I wonder what she did with those diamond cufflinks.

So, I go all in, hoping to salvage this situation.

Buy myself some time.

It's the truth, so maybe I have a chance.

"I came over here with a ring the other day. Thought I should make things official, if I was going to ask you to change your life for me. But then you changed your mind about moving, so I left it in my pocket."

Janice shakes her head in the way a school teacher might

after they caught you cheating on a test. "See? That's exactly what I'm talking about."

"What do you mean?"

"I mean, you're making a marriage proposal conditional! Who does that? If I don't move, then you don't want to spend the rest of your life with me? You'll never be happy until you realize that *you* are the problem, Johnny. Not Honolulu. Not me. *You!* The grass is always greener on the other side of the street. And you're always on the wrong side."

"What are you even talking about?"

"Look at your track record. Moving from here to New York to LA, then back here. Trying to be an actor. Now it's Vegas. What exactly are you looking for?"

This is way too deep a level for me. I didn't know Janice even operated on this level. Part of me doesn't believe it, so I push back. Plus, now she's pissing me off.

"Janice. I'm not the only person in this town thinking about moving because they can't get ahead here. You're in real estate. You know about the cost of housing. We've been over this. So, stop making this about me and admit that you want out. It's fine if you do. Just don't start in with this bullshit psychobabble. Not now."

Rising like a phoenix from the sofa, she points towards the door and says, in a measured tone, "I'd like you to leave. Now."

"Fine," I say.

The first thing I do when I close her apartment door behind me is pull out my phone and accept Linda Chun's friend request.

FIFTEEN

JOHNNY

After I accept Linda's friend request, I decide to put my phone away for the rest of the night and forget about women. I head to a sports bar that serves burgers and fries in red plastic baskets, dripping with grease. The kind of place you can sit and stare into space and mind your own business while people shout at TV screens and eighties rock blares in the background. I sit at the bar and order a beer and a cheeseburger.

Much to my surprise, there's a new bartender. A woman. A smoking hot woman wearing a red spaghetti strap top with lace around the edges and a few tasteful tattoos gracing her slender, bronzed arms.

I am not excited about this. I'm trying to forget about women. I got friendly with this bartender named Carlos, but I guess he's off today, which is one of the reasons I picked this spot. He's cool, the kind of guy you can joke around with. Talk sports or the weather. Get your mind off your problems. Luckily, the hot girl is busy because the bar is packed tonight, and after I get my food, I zone out and we barely interact.

As I drink my beer, I think about what just happened with

Janice. And the more I think about it, the more I think she must have seen me searching up information about Linda Chun. I know that I read one of the articles about Linda's husband and the boating accident when I was at Janice's place, and that was when I was still on the weed. She could have seen me reading it. Stood behind me and read what I was reading. I would not have noticed her doing that.

But why would she have waited this long to pounce?

Is it the fact that I wanted to move to the mainland?

Or the fact that I'm still working as a valet driver, and after two years of dating, I have no plans to change that?

Or is it that I want to end our side hustle? Is that what sparks our flame? The secret we share. The excitement and the rush and the danger of it all. That would be sad, but it could be true.

But then I think about me, and my role in all of this. Why did I hit up Linda Chun in the first place? Why haven't I taken my relationship with Janice to the next level? Why did I pull the plug on the proposal just because she didn't want to move with me? What exactly am I looking for?

It doesn't take a Sigmund Freud to point out that I could have used some counseling when the shit hit the fan, back in high school. When dad got busted and abandoned us, and my mom got sick. I'd had what I'd describe as a great childhood up to that point. Idyllic, even, aside from not having any siblings. It was a little lonely, but Dad filled that role as best he could. My buddy, more than my mentor. I never cried when he left. When my mother died, I did, but not as much as you would think—only a single tear rolling down my cheek at her funeral, which Linda wiped away.

So I pull out my phone again and look at my account to see if Linda has messaged me. She hasn't, which should not surprise me. It's late in California. No texts from Janice either.

The background noise starts to annoy me, so I scarf down my food, slap some cash on the counter, and head home.

———

WHEN I GET HOME, I DM Linda.

How have you been?

Not my best line, but what else can I say after over a decade?

Then I go to my closet and pull out a box.

I don't often let myself do this. The box contains memories, and I'm not normally one to dwell on the past, but it seems appropriate, given that I seem to be at a crossroads. Taking off the lid, I grab the first photo that catches my eye. It's a picture of my dad and me on Christmas Eve when I was seven, during my mom's deployment to Afghanistan. We are at my tutu's house, but it's only the two of us. Dad and me, like it often was. I've got a mile-wide smile on my face because I've talked him into letting me open one of my presents. It's not in the photo, but I remember what it was as if it were yesterday: a Toa Nuva Bionicle. We spent the next few hours working on it.

Then I fish through the box and find a letter. Not the letter I haven't read, but the letter that sits at the bottom of the box, still sealed. A different letter that came in a big, white envelope and gave me the biggest one-two punch of my life. In the letter, I was informed that I'd been accepted to Syracuse University as an acting major. And while it wasn't NYU or USC, it was something. It told me my dreams weren't impossible, in theory. I'd worked hard. I'd gotten accepted. That gave me some short-lived satisfaction.

But that was in theory. In reality, I had a mom with cancer

and a deadbeat dad, and there was no way I could leave her. I didn't even tell mom. Or my tutu. Or anyone, even Linda, except that she found out from my college counselor. Instead, I saved the actual acceptance letter and tossed the rest of the envelope. And tonight, I let myself feel sad about that, which I rarely do. What's the point, right?

At the time, I told myself that college wasn't necessary to be an actor. And it's not. For every Brown University grad who made it to the top of the field, you've got more than a few success stories of people who did it the hard way. Went to New York or LA right out of high school. Worked as waiters or bartenders and took whatever roles they could get. I could do that, I thought. Then I saw an ad for a valet driver, and that became my plan.

And here I am, more than ten years later, still a valet driver and definitely not a successful actor. I have to do something about that, I know. Get myself moving in a better direction.

But what? What direction do I go?

Reaching into the bottom of the box, I take out a letter that's still sealed up and think about opening it. Perhaps it could give me some direction or closure. But no. Tonight is not the night. I tuck it back in the middle of the box among the photos and mementos, put the lid back on, and place it up on a shelf in my closet.

Right as I'm about to call it a night, I see I have a DM from Linda.

> Great to hear from you. I'm working. Let's catch up when I finish my shift. I'll reach out tomorrow.

She doesn't say where she's working, but I find it odd. She's working the night shift? Sounds a little desperate. I thought she got a lot of money when her husband died. Well, since I've struck out with women, I turn on the TV.

I'm not tired, but I want to be. It's one of those days that needs to get behind me so I can move forward. Exactly the kind of day that keeps me up at night. I search for something on Netflix, and try not to think about the fact that I still have some weed in my nightstand drawer.

Billy Jack.

I haven't seen that film in ages. Dad made me watch it back in the day. It's about a Vietnam vet who defends women's honor and fights for the oppressed.

"Now there's a hero for you," Dad said, as Billy Jack got hauled off to prison for his vigilante justice at the end of the movie. I learned two critical things from that film. One was that the law isn't always on the right side of a situation.

The other was, if you're going to even the score and met out some vigilante justice, do it quietly.

SIXTEEN

JOHNNY

I think the worst is over with the weed withdrawal, but I still took a Tylenol PM to make sure I got some decent sleep. Nothing worse than a bad night's sleep when you're trying to catch a serial killer and clear yourself of a potential murder charge.

So, here I am, trudging over to a job I tolerate after a not very productive two days off, with no girlfriend and no plan, knowing that it's time I got my shit together. It was time a few years ago, but I think everyone in my generation is a few years behind schedule. But if the last few years are any indication, I'll be forty before I know it. Then in a flash, I'll be Leo, with more of my life behind me than ahead of me.

Not that there's anything terrible about being Leo. But I wanted more from life. Plus, Leo inherited a paid-off house worth a million dollars, even in its shabby condition. So, I'd be Leo, minus the net worth.

Taking a deep breath, I head to the valet desk and see Mandy, who works the front desk, standing where Tina should be. I was actually looking forward to picking Tina's brain a little about Derek Anderson, so I'm disappointed. I'm pretty sure she was supposed to work today, and she said nothing about a vacation. Maybe she's sick.

"Where's Tina," I ask.

Mandy rolls her eyes. "That's the million-dollar question."

"What do you mean?"

"I mean, she didn't show up. We've called and called. Her phone goes straight to voicemail. We pulled in a replacement, but he's not here yet. Thankfully, it's not that busy now."

My mind flashes to Derek Anderson chatting up Tina, and my stomach tenses.

"That's not like her. What if something happened to her?"

"That's above my pay grade," Mandy says.

"Pretty harsh, Mandy," I say. "What if that ex of hers did something?"

"Don't worry about Tina," Mandy says, rolling her eyes. "She's a drama queen. She's fine." Then she leaves me to attend to some front desk computer glitch while things are still slow.

Leo steps up to the valet desk, and I fill him in on the fact that Tina's a no-show. He'll work behind the desk until Tina or a replacement shows up.

"Remember that husband of hers? How he came here, all crazed that day?" I remind him.

Leo's brow furrows, as if this makes no sense to him. "What about him?"

"Maybe he came back," I offer.

"That seems a little premature," Leo says. "It's only been a few hours. She could have overslept."

"Tina's been off for two days," I point out. "She lives alone. Maybe it hasn't been a few hours. Maybe it's been a few days."

Leo shrugs. "She hasn't said much about her ex lately. She's probably fine."

"She was talking to Derek Anderson," I tell him.

"The Tesla guy? What's with you and the Tesla guy?"

"Nothing," I say. "It's just, he was with Lani Lum. She's dead. He was chatting up Tina. Now Tina's missing."

"Tina's not missing. She's late for work."

"Let's hope so."

And now I wonder why Leo's not more concerned.

"Johnny. The reason you're so concerned about this Tesla guy. It wouldn't have to do with something you found in his car when you were sitting in it that day, now would it?"

Crap. Crap. Crap.

Could things possibly get any worse?

"I don't know what you're talking about," I offer. But my delivery is weak, mirroring my excuse, and we both know it.

"You know exactly what I'm talking about, and don't worry. I'm not a rat. But if you know something that might stop women from getting killed and you don't tell someone about it, well, that makes you something far worse than a petty criminal."

"I looked around a little, okay? I am not a petty criminal. I was curious to know if it was his car or if he was a tourist. And there was nothing suspicious in the car."

This is true, and Leo seems to buy at least this part of my story.

"Then what is it you don't like about the guy?"

"It's a feeling," I say. "He seems like the Ted Bundy type."

"Or he's a guy who's doing better than you and you don't like it."

I shrug. "Perhaps."

"Johnny. If something's missing from your life, go find it. But you're not going to find it snooping around in people's cars and playing amateur detective."

Seems to be a familiar theme.

A car drives up, and I grab it, leaving Leo and his words of wisdom hanging in the air as I drive the vehicle to the garage and think about how to get my life on a better track.

SEVENTEEN
JOHNNY

My shift is ending when I look up to see the detective from the news broadcast stroll up to the valet stand. Immediately, I recognize her. I have an uncanny ability to remember people's faces, even if I've only seen them once or twice. Over the years, I've learned to sometimes keep it to myself, because people can find it odd, like I've been studying them in a creepy way. It's not like that, it's a skill I have, but I can see how it would be off-putting, especially for women.

Her name I don't recall. Just the face, taking questions on the news broadcast. She saunters over to me.

Why me?

"I'm Detective Akana," she says. "Can we have a chat?"

"Sure," I say, wishing I'd taken Uncle Mel's advice and called an attorney. I hope Janice didn't do something rash, like hand over those diamond cufflinks and tell them I broke into Derek Anderson's house. Or maybe Leo told someone about his suspicions. That would be easier to explain.

But soon I realize it's not about either of those things.

It's something potentially much worse.

"We wanted to ask you about Shayna McCarthy," she says. "Do you know who she is?"

My eyes widen.

Me? Why me?

"Sure," I say. "But I've never seen the woman in my life."

Is this part of a general sweep?

But I know they've already done that.

And I've already told them I didn't see her.

Calm down, I tell myself. This is actually better than asking me about Lani Lum, because there's nothing to lie about. I don't know Shayna McCarthy. Never laid eyes on the woman, in fact. Maybe they're asking everyone again. They've known all along she was here the week before she disappeared, but now there are two dead women connected to the Royal.

"I heard about it on the news," I say. "No, wait. I heard about it from my coworker, Tina."

"Your coworker who didn't show up today."

"Yeah. Any more on that?"

She narrows her eyes at me, as if to tell me this is a one-way street in terms of questions. "Did you have any interaction with Shayna McCarthy when she was here for her bachelorette weekend?"

"Me? No. I didn't see her."

"You sound pretty sure about that."

"I am. I never forget a face. Like yours. I recognized you from the news, right away."

Detective Akana has a commanding presence. She's measured and composed. Not a fidget or a twitch about her. Her stillness is unnerving, and I wonder if it's a tactic. "Yes. I could tell. You seem to be keeping quite an eye on this case."

"Along with everyone else in Honolulu."

She looks me up and down, then continues. "So. You didn't interact with Shayna McCarthy at all that weekend?"

"No. I did not. I was only here one of the days, and then I was off."

Detective Akana nods. "Where do you sit on your breaks, Mr. Silva?"

My brow furrows. "Where do I sit?"

"It's a pretty direct question, but if you need clarification, I can provide it." The hint of a smile on her face taunts me.

Rolling my eyes, I continue. "If it's overcast, I go to the park. If it's a weekend and there's no conferences, I sit down by the conference rooms. If there's a conference, we have to go to the break room."

"And where did you take your breaks that day?"

Shrugging, I tell her. "I don't remember."

She leans in. "Let me jog your memory. You took your break near the conference rooms. And Shayna McCarthy was also seen in the vicinity around the time you were on your break."

"So?"

"So, you're telling me you still don't remember seeing her?"

"I'm telling you that I did not see her. I'd remember her face if I'd seen her."

"Because you have a great memory for faces."

"Right."

"Yet you didn't remember Lani Lum's face when your co-worker showed you her photo on the phone screen."

Letting a huff slip out, I say, "I already told the other cop. There was a glare on Tina's phone."

"And now Tina's missing. Where were you last night, Mr. Silva?"

I don't like where this is going.

I tell her I was at my girlfriend's and then I went to a bar.

"With your girlfriend?"

"No. By myself."

"Do you have a receipt from the establishment?"

"No," I tell her. "I paid in cash, from my tips."

She nods along, the corners of her mouth lifting ever so slightly. She's starting to enjoy making me sweat. "Did you talk to anyone there? Anyone who could corroborate your claim?"

I don't hold out much hope of the bartender remembering me. But still, I describe the woman, leaving out the hot part. And I almost laugh out loud at the irony. The one time I don't chat up a hot woman, it counts against me. Seems like I can't win for trying these days.

But then I remember something.

Something that could be important.

"Did anyone tell you that Tina was flirting with Derek Anderson a few days ago? He's the same guy who had lunch with Lani Lum. Why don't you go talk to him?"

"Did that piss you off?" she asks, like Officer Yoshimura before her, trying to rile me. I guess they talk.

Playing dumb, I ask, "Did what piss me off?"

"Tina, flirting with the rich haole guy? Maybe you like Tina. Maybe you liked Lani Lum, too."

Rolling my eyes, I decide being passive isn't the way to go. I heard once that innocent people protest, and I'm innocent of these murders. "You're barking up the wrong tree, Detective. But that doesn't matter, does it? Smooth talker like Derek Anderson. Maybe he sweet-talked you, too."

"Really got it in for the guy, don't you?"

"Maybe it's mutual. Is he the one who says I was sitting near her? Got any video footage to back up that claim?"

Detective Akana's jaw stiffens, and that's telling. Maybe Derek Anderson's trying to set me up. If so, I need to get ahead of it. I also have a feeling there's no footage. It's only backed up for a week or so. It's probably gone by now.

"That'll be all for now," she says.

She stands and goes on her way, leaving me shaking in my boots, although it's pushing ninety today and muggy as hell, and of course, I'm not wearing boots. At least I'm not sweating. Because it's the truth. I've never seen Shayna McCarthy in my life.

Two things occur to me, though.

I need to get an attorney.

And I need to get something on Derek Anderson.

Something solid, that I can take to the cops.

Before he plants something on me that lands me in prison.

EIGHTEEN

JOHNNY

I haven't heard from Janice since I left her place two days ago, but I have heard a lot from Linda Chun. She's living in San Diego, working as a nurse. This doesn't surprise me. As I said, she was the caregiver type, back when we dated. When we were young, she wasn't that interested in college. It was too expensive, she claimed. And like mine, her family didn't have much money.

But the guy she married had money, so it gave her a chance to go back to school and launch her career. He had kids from another marriage, and Linda became an instant stepmom. When I asked if she still sees the kids now that he's passed on, she didn't answer me. Maybe it's still too painful to talk about. From their social media photos, it looks like they were a happy family.

We were on a DM roll, but now she's pulled back a little, and that's fine. It could be that she reached out to me in a wave of nostalgia and grief, and now she's realized that she's not ready yet. It's not even been a year since her husband's death. And I'm not even officially broken up with Janice. For me, this has been a nice distraction from my real problem: the fact that I might have a serial killer trying to frame me for murder.

So, I look up from my phone towards the house of my nemesis, where I sit across the street from it in my Honda Accord, wondering if I should risk breaking in one more time to snap a photo of those shoes. I'm thinking that if he's keeping women's shoes as a trophy, the police might be able to match the women's shoes in his closet to the missing ones of the two murder victims, and then, at the very least, I could mail in a photo as an anonymous tip.

I've been trying to determine if there's a pattern to when he comes and goes, but so far, I've had no luck. It's just getting dark, and he left about fifteen minutes ago, wearing a dress aloha shirt and slacks, as if he was going out on the town. If he was running to the store, he'd probably be in shorts and a t-shirt. So, if I'm going to do it, now is the time.

A rap on my car window startles me, and my stomach lurches. The phone drops from my hand as it dawns on me that the cops could be watching his house.

But I look up to see a guy a little younger than me wearing a Green Day t-shirt. He doesn't look like a plainclothes detective. More like a gamer, thin and pale, like he spends a lot of time indoors. His sandy brown hair is a little too long in the front, and wire-rimmed glasses sit on the bridge of his nose.

Before I know it, I'm sitting at the Starbucks in Aina Haina, talking to Sam Sanders, a true crime podcaster following the case. He's from Seattle, which explains the complexion. Nobody from Honolulu could be that pale.

Sam seems to know more about the case than the cops. For example, the police haven't released the exact cause of death in either homicide, although they said it was an "apparent drug overdose." It was Janice who first claimed that Lani Lum died from an insulin overdose, but police have not confirmed that.

But Sanders seems to believe that it's true, and he tells me that Shayna McCarthy also died of an insulin overdose.

I don't see how he could know this if my Uncle Mel didn't, so it makes me skeptical of him, Janice, and all these true crime fanatics. And suddenly, I start to laugh. At myself, really. For deluding myself into thinking I could solve this case by breaking into Derek Anderson's house instead of going to an attorney, as Mel suggested, and covering my own ass.

"What's so funny?" Sam asks me.

I shake my head. "Nothing. I'm just a little overwhelmed."

"So, why were you sitting in front of Derek Anderson's house?"

"I told you. I saw him talking to Lani Lum at the Royal. And then I saw him talking to my coworker, Tina, the other day. And then Tina didn't show up for work."

"Yeah. So you said. But you told me your coworker texted your supervisor later that day and told everyone she had to go out of town to see a sick relative."

Shrugging, I tell him a partial truth. "I don't like the guy, okay? He gives me a vibe."

"A serial killer vibe?"

"Maybe. A douchebag vibe for sure."

With that, Sam chuckles a little. "Yeah, I get that."

After a pointed pause, he gives me a hard stare. "I know there's something you're not telling me. I also know that you're a person of interest in this case."

My stomach sinks because that part is true, according to Mel. Maybe this guy has someone on the inside. Maybe this Sam Sanders could be useful to me.

"You can't possibly know for sure any of what you said," I tell him.

"Fair point. I'm ninety-nine percent sure that my source is solid. This isn't a hobby to me, Johnny. I'm good at what I do. I make a lot of money at it. And I'm serious as a heart attack about getting something on this case that'll blow up my brand. So, if there's something you want to tell me, I'm listening, and so are my nearly two million subscribers. If you're innocent, instead of hiding in the shadows casing Anderson's house like a psychopath, you could shine a light on the truth."

"I don't know what the truth is. It's just a feeling. And why would anyone believe me?"

"I've been investigating the case. I believe you. I don't think it was you. But I don't think it was Derek Anderson either."

"Why is that?" he says.

"Because. I think it's a woman."

"A woman? Isn't that pretty rare?"

"Yeah. Except maybe not. Women are more subtle. More insidious, if you will. They don't like to get up close and personal with their victims. Poisonings. Drug overdoses. Under the radar stuff. Maybe they're just better at getting away with murder."

Blowing out a breath, I say, "Why? What would the motive be?"

"With male serial killers, it's much more varied. Fetishes. Gripes against women. Power. Control, which they lack in other areas of their lives. But with women, it's pretty consistent. Love or money. Black widows, who murder for the cash. Or the jealous types, taking out their aggression on actual victims or proxies."

"So you're convinced it's a woman?" I ask him.

With an air of authority that looks ridiculous on his baby face, he says "I am."

"What if it's a man who wants you to think it's a woman? It would be the perfect crime, wouldn't it? Leading everyone down the wrong path?"

He smiles. "A man. Like you, for instance, Johnny Boy?" he says. "Serial killers often insert themselves into investigations."

"Nobody's more inserted into this investigation than you are, Sammie Boy."

The snipe felt good, but the instant gratification is short-lived. I don't need any enemies, and this guy can make a lot of them for me. I should learn to keep my smart mouth shut.

But he seems nonplussed. Excited, even, his eyes wide with wonder. "You know what, Johnny Silva?"

"What?"

"This?" He motions between us. "What we've got going here? It's pure gold. Listeners love this kind of back-and-forth. You'd be great on air with me. That voice of yours. It's so resonant. So commanding."

He's not shining me on. I know this about myself, which is why I was successful at voice acting, and I tell him this. And I have to say, his voice doesn't match his baby looks. It's smooth and pleasant, with a nice cadence; the register is a little higher than mine. It's an easy voice on the ears. We'd make a good team.

"I've been looking for a female co-host, but the bro thing works great too. What do you say we give it a shot? We could try it for this case, and then go from there."

"I'll think about it," I say, although it's a crazy idea.

But why close a door?

First, I'll contact the attorney Mel recommended, who I'm sure will tell me I'm out of my mind.

"Don't think too long," he says. "I don't give out these kinds of offers very often. Now. Let's drill down on our list of suspects. Know any jealous women with a connection to the Royal or the two victims?"

My mind flashes to Janice, checking up on me at work. Maybe she's the one who saw me sitting near Shayna

McCarthy. Perhaps she saw me staring at Lani Lum that day she was at the Royal. Far-fetched, but stranger things have happened. I doubt she's a serial killer, but she could be the one trying to mess with me. I'm not ready to trust Sam, though, or to throw Janice under the bus, so I keep this to myself.

"I'll think on it," I say.

But of course, I'll do more than think about it.

Because I need to get my hands on those diamond cufflinks, and I need to find out if Janice really is holding a grudge against me.

NINETEEN
JOHNNY

I've been thinking about my dad a lot lately. Maybe it was the visit with Uncle Mel. Or maybe it's the reconnection with Linda Chun. But whatever it is, he's been on my mind.

When I was little, Dad was my hero. My go-to guy. Mom was the heavy. The one who put me in time-outs when I was a toddler and grounded me as a teen when I deserved it. Dad was the fun parent. The one who could get my mom to lighten up and crack a smile, or shoot me a wink when I trudged off to my room after one of her admonitions, like we were sharing a little secret. They had a good marriage, don't get me wrong. But my mom, being military, believed in the chain of command. Rules comforted her.

"If you break rules in the military," she said to me once, "people die." Dad let out a guffaw at that one, and she made him sleep on the couch that night. That was them, and it was fine—until it all went to hell.

Janice knows me better than most people, and I have to admit that it's weighing on me - what she said about the grass being greener on the other side. Am I a dreaming drifter, or is there more to it? Even with acting, I didn't try that hard. You have to be relentless to make it in a field like that, and I've been anything but relentless.

Dad supported my acting hobby. Mom thought it was a waste of time, but they both came to my school plays and humored me. Or when Mom was deployed, Dad came with my tutu. And when my dad got arrested, I felt betrayed. Then mom got sick, and the anger came. At him, for leaving us. At her for getting sick in the first place, although that was totally irrational. And finally, I felt anger at myself for letting my father die without granting him my forgiveness, which he'd asked for many times.

Now I can see that I'm too old to blame my life choices on my parents or my circumstances. I could have buckled down in New York instead of abandoning stage acting for Hollywood when things got tough. I could have taken parts as an extra and paid my dues in LA, instead of growing restless and heading back to Honolulu with my tail between my legs. And now, instead of fixing what's broken, I'm once again thinking about moving.

So perhaps that's why I'm letting my mind run wild with the notion of becoming a successful true crime podcaster. Solving this case. Moving my life in a positive direction. And, of course, eliminating myself as a murder suspect.

Yes, maybe Janice had a point about the grass is greener thing, so that will be my opening offering in my attempt to determine if she's trying to set me up for murder.

***

"THANKS FOR AGREEING to talk to me," I say.

It's Friday. My day off, and we're at a coffee shop in Kaimuki near where she lives. It's been nearly a week since I've seen her or talked to her. We've never been out of touch this long. I didn't ask to meet at her place, and she didn't offer. "I've missed you, Jan."

Janice rolls her eyes. "Let's not do this. What did you want to talk about?" She takes a sip of her iced latte, secure in the fact that she's holding the cards.

"I've been thinking about what you said," I tell her.

"Can you be more specific?"

"About the grass is greener stuff. You might have a point."

She leans back and crosses her arms. "Go on."

"Go on?"

Her eyes widen. "Elaborate."

"I mean, what you said about me moving around all the time. New York. LA. Now Vegas. You might have a point."

"And?"

"And I wanted to let you know I've been giving it some thought. Maybe moving isn't the answer. Maybe I need to take charge of my life. Do something different."

"For example?"

I don't want to tell her about the podcasting gig yet, or that I was staking out Derek Anderson's house. Hoping this will please her, I say, "I don't know yet. Maybe I could make a move into management at the resort."

She suggested this two years ago when we first met, and it's always a possibility. They like to promote from within. The GM, in fact, started out in reservations. But I never wanted to work in hospitality. It's always been a stepping stone for me, and moving into a better position seems like giving up on my dreams.

"All of a sudden, this dawns on you? I said that two years ago." Her look is stern. Skeptical, even. I wonder what's going on in that mind of hers, or why this doesn't please her at all.

"Yeah, well, you had a point, babe. And it was a crappy

move to pull back on my proposal when you changed your mind about moving."

She's still not showing any signs of thawing out, and I have a sinking feeling there's more to this than I know. After an awkward pause, with her deep brown eyes still trained on me, she says, "And that's all you wanted to tell me?"

"Um, yeah. I mean, that's the gist of it."

She places her hands on the table and leans in. "You. Are. Unbelievable,"

"What's that supposed to mean?"

"Why don't you go ask Linda Chun!" Janice thunders.

With that, she grabs her iced latte, pushes up on the table and storms off, knocking over my coffee in the process, partially onto my lap. Thankfully, it's not boiling hot, but it's warm enough to jolt me—and leave me with a growing wet patch creeping towards my groin area.

Heads turn to look at me and I shrug, wondering once again what she's planning to do with those diamond cufflinks, and wishing I'd opened with that.

TWENTY

JOHNNY

Grabbing a coffee in the break room before my shift, I look around for Leo. He's been off for a few days, and I need to get a read on him. I'm dying to talk to Tina about her chat with Derek Anderson, too, but she's taken a week off from work to care for some sick relative in California.

The thing is, I called her, and it goes straight to voicemail, and I have a sinking feeling that something's wrong. I don't know her all that well, but I distinctly remember that when she was having trouble with her husband, I asked her if there was a family member who could help her out. Someone she could stay with, preferably off island. She told me she didn't have much family.

Now, it's possible that a woman like Tina would help a family member who wouldn't help her. But still, it seems a little fishy to me. And why wouldn't she be answering her cell phone? So, my mind is running wild with theories. Theories about Derek Anderson.

Was Tina getting too close to the situation?

Did he abduct her and get her to text and ask for the time off?

Or did he somehow access her phone and send the texts himself?

And I'm considering once again breaking into Anderson's house, in the off chance he's holding Tina there. At the very least, I could snap a photo of those shoes. I'm not sure how Sam Sanders will play into all of this, but I'm sure he could be useful to me.

On my way out to the valet desk, I spot Leo. We haven't talked since that cop questioned me about Shayna McCarthy. I wonder if they questioned Leo again, and I ask him.

"I shouldn't be talking to you," he says.

"What? Why not?"

"Johnny? Are you dim? What do you mean, why not? You're radioactive, that's why not."

"What the hell does that mean?"

"It means you're a person of interest. They're looking hard at you. I know I said I wasn't a rat, but that was when we were talking about petty theft. This is a murder investigation."

Is that why Tina's not picking up my calls?

Because I'm radioactive?

"You can't possibly think that I'm a serial killer!"

Leo shakes his head. "Of course I don't think that. I don't need them poking around in my business. Guilt by association, you know?"

"You got something to hide?" I ask.

He shoots daggers at me. "Don't throw this back on me. I know you've been up to something, and I was willing to look the other way. But not now. I didn't tell them you were looking in the guy's files, but I should have. Get an attorney, Johnny. Come clean. The more lies they catch you in, the more guilty you'll seem."

I try to change the subject. "I'm worried about Tina. I tried calling her, and her phone went right to voicemail. Remember when he was chatting her up? And he may have been the last person to see Lani Lum."

"Again with you and the Derek Anderson guy? She texted our boss. She's in California."

"Yeah, well, according to Tina, she didn't have much family. Now, all of a sudden, she goes to California to care for some sick relative who wouldn't help her when she was with an abusive guy? Maybe her ex-husband did something to her. Maybe he's holding her hostage somewhere, and he made her send that text. Maybe she went into hiding. Why isn't she answering her phone? Why isn't it even turned on? And why doesn't anybody but me seem to care about this?"

"Tina is not my problem. And if you know what's good for you, you won't make her your problem either. Get an attorney, Johnny Boy. Keep your head down. Stop poking around in the investigation and Derek Anderson's life. It's a commonly known fact that serial killers sometimes try to insert themselves into the investigation."

"Hey, Leo. You're hands ain't so clean. You have a connection to these two women, too. Even more of one than I do. You got Lani Lum's car, not me. Maybe you did remember her and you kept your mouth shut about it."

"What the hell is wrong with you, Silva? Even with the cops looking at you, I'm not willing to go there, but you are?" Leo shakes his head and looks at me like I'm vermin. Then he holds up a hand, he says, "Stay away from me, Johnny. Far away."

With that, I've officially pissed off another person who used to be in my camp. Maybe Janice and Leo will gang up on me and turn me in to the cops. Really put a nail in my coffin.

I get why he's avoiding me, but why isn't he more

concerned about Tina and her disappearance? Maybe because there's always been a bit of friction between Tina and Leo. He thought she was the type to exaggerate. That her claims about the husband were overblown.

But then he can be a bit of a chauvinist. Janice would call Leo a misogynist if she knew some of the things he's said, but I think that's an overused word. But his attitudes about women are at odds with the present generation, and even his own.

Tina told me that he was inappropriate with her a few times, making comments about her looks or her clothing. Women these days can be overly sensitive, though, so I didn't give it much weight. But I guess that would explain his lack of concern about her whereabouts. I wonder if she ever complained to management about it. That would surely piss Leo off.

Which brings me back to my original question.

Where is Tina?

Like a lightning bolt, an idea strikes me.

I pull up my phone and text Sam Sanders.

And I'm pretty sure it's a great one.

Sam and I stand at the front door of Derek Anderson's Aina Haina residence.

I turn to Sam and he says, "You do it."

No we are not breaking in. We're here to do a spotlight interview for our upcoming podcast episode: *Where's Tina?*

Sam loved my idea. Drill down on the fact that Tina isn't answering her phone and it's going straight to voicemail. Force the cops to take her potential disappearance more seriously. Talk about her ex, the stalker. Interview people who were seen with her.

People like Derek Anderson.

Then bring up the other murdered women, and their connection to him and the Royal. Stop short of accusing him. Get him to open the door. Invite us in. Get a read.

I can hear it playing out in my head. Much better than another break-in.

Shrugging, I knock.

Nothing.

Then I knock again, harder this time, rap-rap-raping to no

avail, which is strange. A light in the upstairs window and his car in the driveway indicate that he's home.

My mind flashes to those crime shows where the cops arrive at the house and the suspect darts out the back door. And I could kick myself, because one of us should have thought of that, and it probably should've been me. If he saw us and bolted, maybe I'm actually on to something.

"Sam," I say. "What if he slipped out the back door?"

Sam's eyes widen. "You stay here," he says. I'll go around back and check."

Darting my head around, I see if I can catch a glimpse of our potential fugitive. I stopped knocking because it seems futile. And then it dawns on me that somebody could've picked him up. Maybe he's not even here. Maybe I'm getting too caught up in all this true crime stuff.

Then a blood-curdling scream coming from the back of the house rips through me. It's so visceral, the hairs on the back of my neck stand up, and I swear, I feel a stabbing sensation in my gut, which I'm sure is my nerves seizing up on me. And suddenly, this isn't a joke anymore.

What if he's got Sam?

What if he killed Sam?

I probably should call 9-1-1, but there's no time to fumble with my phone, so I run around back as fast as I can, thinking I'll help Sam first and call later. In a flash, I see Sam holding onto the frame of the door opening, but I can't see his face. He's leaning on it, like he's having trouble standing. At least he's alive.

Is he hurt?

Shot?

Stabbed?

"Sam," I call out.

"I'm okay," he says.

Then he leans over and pukes.

My mind is reeling.

Did he find Tina's dead body?

Did we actually catch a serial killer?

Running up to him, I say, "What is it? Did you find Tina?"

Shaking his head, he says, "Anderson's not our killer."

"Huh? How do you know?"

"Because Anderson's dead. And from the smell in there, it seems like he's been dead for a while now."

My eyes nearly pop out of my head. This turns everything upside down. All the bits of information I had pieced together are now dumped out on the table, and maybe even spilled on the floor; all the clues, ideas, and suspects now a scrambled mess of confusion.

"What does this mean?" I ask.

Sam is still processing, and from the look on his face, I almost don't want to ask this question because who knows what kind of horror sits inside that house?

"Is he... intact?" I ask.

"Yeah. It's not that bad. It's the stench. It looks like he was shot."

"Wait. How did you get in?"

"The back door was open. I smelled something, so I went in."

"What do we do now?"

"We call the cops," he says.

"Okay but first let me go take a look around."

"Are you crazy? There's been a murder. I can justify walking in and finding him with that smell and the open back door, but not poking around upstairs. He's right there," Sam gestures to his right, "in the living room."

"They don't need to know."

"What about your prints and DNA?"

"Don't worry," I say, taking off my t-shirt as I shoot past him. "I'll cover my hand if I have to touch anything."

Blazing past him into the house and up the stairs before he can stop me, I open the closet and snap a few photos of the shoes. But that's not the real reason I'm up here. With Anderson dead, the investigators are sure to comb through the house, and I need a reason to have been up here if they find my prints or DNA from the burglary. I've got a witness now that can attest to the fact that all I did was run up here to poke around and see what I could find for the podcast. Stupid thing to do, sure, but something that would result in a slap on the wrist, at worst. Better than a B&E charge.

"Okay," I say when I'm back outside. "Call them. By the way, there were women's shoes in his closet. And those women were found with no shoes."

"Just shoes and nothing else?"

"No clothes," I say. "Just shoes. And some make-up and jewelry in the bathroom drawer."

By now, Sam has regained his composure. He turns to me and says with a grin, "This is gonna be epic, isn't it?"

Nodding my head, I say, "Yeah. Epic."

And then it's my turn to hurl.

TWENTY-TWO
JOHNNY

After three hours of relentless questioning, I'm finally home. I'm too charged up to sleep though, so I'm sipping a beer on my lanai, looking out at Diamond Head.

There's a full moon tonight, and it looks almost surreal, hanging above the volcanic peaks like a stage prop. I would call it magical or romantic under different circumstances, but tonight it looks ominous. Spooky, even.

It reminds me of a B-movie my dad used to love that was filmed at the old Coco Palms on Kaua'i, about a group of flight attendants who get stuck there with a werewolf. *Killer Moon* or something? I can't remember, and for some strange reason, this is what's important to me right now, so I search it up.

Deathmoon.

Yeah. That's it.

A nice memory. It reminds me of better times with my dad. He was into those old horror flicks, the ones that were more about mood than gore. Me, I watched for the bonding and the nostalgia. Dad went on and on about how it was, back in the day. Coco Palms was classic old Hawai'i of the Elvis variety, razed to the ground by Hurricane Iniki in the nineties, its fate still in limbo.

Perhaps Kaua'i is on my mind because that was our next steps. Sam and me. We were planning on going over on my day off to poke around. He found an aunt of Tina's who lives over there and thought maybe Tina went there to hide out, that California was a diversion. We got strict instructions from the cops to stay out of the case, though, and I think we should listen to them. At least, I plan to listen to the police. Sam can do what he wants.

Linda Chun finally messaged me back, I notice. I wonder if this is a sign. A sign that going back in time is somehow the key to my getting my life together. Or perhaps there's something to that grass is greener thing. Maybe it extends back and forth across the decades, too. What do I know about how it was, back in the day? Maybe it sucked worse then than now. I couldn't have reunited with Linda over a social media app in the seventies, that's for sure.

In her message, she apologizes for the delay, informing me that she'd been seeing a guy, and it felt like a violation to keep messaging me. Then she tells me they broke up. And now I feel like a perfect shit for hitting her up while I was still with Janice. She's a better person than me. Always was.

I send her something short and sweet. She's fast asleep, I'm sure:

> No explanations needed. It's always a
> pleasure to hear from you.

The interrogation went better than I expected. I said nothing about running upstairs to get the photos of the shoes, and neither did Sam. In truth, they never asked me. I got very lucky, because they asked me nothing I needed to lie about. It was the same guy who came to the Royal. Officer Yoshimura, not the woman. Not the lead detective on the case. The shot was back of the head, execution style. Which means he didn't see it coming. The questions were easy to answer. I didn't have to lie.

What were you doing at Derek Anderson's house?
Did you touch the body?
Did you know Lani Lum?
Did you know Shayna McCarthy?
Are you obsessed with Tina Fernandez?

"Why are you so unconcerned about Tina Fernandez?" I shot back. "Her phone goes straight to voicemail. Eight years she's worked at the Royal, and she's never taken time off from work with no advance notice. She told me she had no relatives. And she had a violent, stalker ex-husband who personally got in my face at work. There's a record of that."

"Yes. We know," Officer Yoshimura said.

"Maybe her disappearance has nothing to do with the other women. Maybe her ex did something to her. He could have gotten into her phone and sent those texts. But I'm telling you, something's not right."

"Your coworker Leo Sanchez thinks you have an overactive imagination. He's not too concerned about Tina. Said she's prone to exaggeration."

I let out a breath, grateful for the fact that Leo didn't tell them I was lingering in Anderson's car. But then something dawned on me, and I felt the color drain from my face. It wasn't lost on the officer.

"What is it?" he asked.

"Nothing," I said. "His attitudes towards women are a little dated, that's all."

Yoshimura let it go, but not before jotting something down.

I hadn't planned to throw Leo under the bus, especially since he has something on me and apparently, he didn't use it. I didn't tell the officer what crossed my mind, because I don't need Leo retaliating until I figure out if it means anything. If the cause of death really was an insulin overdose.

Because Leo's mother is diabetic. And he sure has an attitude towards women, especially the good-looking ones he refers to as "stuck up." But how does Derek Anderson's murder figure into this, if at all? Maybe Leo offed Anderson out of jealousy, because he had more success with Tina? That seems far-fetched. Maybe Anderson has enemies who have nothing to do with the women. I'll talk it over with Sam.

Sam, who's convinced the killer is a woman.

I finally got that attorney lined up. We're meeting tomorrow, and I'm going to tell him about the break-in. Figure out my worst-case scenario. Leo can't prove I did anything illegal in Anderson's car. He's not a real threat. But Janice, she has the cufflinks. And you know what they say about a woman scorned.

Could Janice, with her jealous streak, have ...

My phone dings with an alert, saving me from going down a rabbit hole better left unexplored. It's from Linda Chun. Why is she up this late? Or early? It'd be four in the morning in Cali.

> I'm coming for a visit next week. I'd love to catch up.

Looks like it's time to get some clarity on my relationship status with Janice and figure out what's going on in that mind of hers.

How did she know about Linda and me?

Was she spying on me at work?

Did that comment about Tina mean anything?

The rabbit hole beckons me.

I dive in.

"What did you say?" I ask Sam.

It's morning, the day after we found Derek Anderson dead, and I don't work today. I'm home, about to head over to the attorney's office, but we decided to check in with each other first about next steps, since we didn't get too much time to talk things over last night.

"I said, I overheard them saying Anderson's murder might not be related to the serial killings."

"Yes, but what was that last part? About a burglary?"

"They said his house was burglarized. He reported a pair of diamond cufflinks stolen and filed an insurance claim, a few weeks ago."

I'm glad we're not talking face-to-face, because my jaw is on the floor. The cops wouldn't have done much of anything for a petty burglary, but now that there's been a homicide, they'll go back to that night again. Look for video footage from the neighbors. Interview people. I need to talk to Janice. Maybe we need to come clean and get ahead of it.

"I'm going over to Kaua'i, Sam says. "I got the address of

Tina's aunt who lives there. I want the element of surprise, so I'm—"

"Sure, sure," I say. "I'm late. Gotta go."

I guess it's a good time to be meeting with an attorney. While I'm getting strapped in, I quick tell Siri to call Janice. She doesn't pick up, but I leave a message as I'm backing out of my parking space.

"Call me," I say. "It's urgent. Really urgent."

SOON, I'm sitting in the lobby of a suite of offices in downtown Honolulu, on Queen Street between Bishop and Alakea, waiting for Marcus Snyder, Honolulu's premier defense attorney. He's got a reputation as an unscrupulous shark, willing to do anything to get his client an acquittal. When Mel recommended him, I hesitated, because I feel like if you hire this guy, it looks like you have something to hide.

But still, I can't argue with his track record.

Soon, he greets me. He's confident and commanding, with short, wavy hair that has mostly turned gray. His beady eyes reflect an intensity that works in the courtroom. They scream *there's your reasonable doubt, people!*

I tell him everything about Derek Anderson and Janice and me, and he barely blinks. He's represented murders. Corporate criminals. Rapists. A petty burglary does not phase a guy like him, even if it's attached to a homicide.

"So you didn't kill the guy," Marcus says. "Or the women. Is that what I'm hearing? You just broke in and took a pair of cufflinks?"

"To be clear, my girlfriend took the cufflinks. I didn't know about it until later. But yes, I broke in. But I still feel he's connected to the murders of those two women and my coworker's disappearance. I don't know how."

"That's not your problem and it's not my problem. Now, I'm going to the cops to get everything they have about the case. Best thing is, we clear you for the nights of the murders. They must have time of death by now. And if the burglary comes up, it comes up. Worst case, you get a year or two. More likely, probation and community service."

"Should I get ahead of it? Make a deal? Tell them what I know?"

"Are you out of your mind? No. Now, go home or wherever it is you have to be. Stop playing amateur detective. Let me do my job. Is there anything to this bar fight on your record?"

"What do you mean?"

"Anything I should know that could come up?"

"Why would that come up?"

"It might be why they're looking at you, in particular."

"He assaulted me," I say. "I was the victim."

"Yeah. I see the charges were dismissed when you dropped them. But he's dead now. That might not look good."

"Dead? That had nothing to do with me. How'd he die?"

"Hiking on an unmarked trail on the North Shore, a year or so later."

I shrug. "One less wife beater in the world."

The guy had a rap sheet a mile long, and not only for domestic violence. Attempted murder, for one, which I'm sure Snyder knows. At this comment, Marcus Snyder smiles. I think it's the first thing I said that's made him have an ounce of respect for me.

"What do I owe you?" I ask.

"For now, we're square. Mel paid my retainer. We go way back," he says. "Gave him my friends and family rate."

Shrugging, I start to ask about my podcast gig, and if he thinks it's a good idea, but he cuts me off.

"What part of 'go' didn't you understand?"

As I'm leaving, I see a giant of a man sitting in the lobby wearing a plain white t-shirt and a pair of jeans, staring down at his rubber slippers. When I get a glimpse of his face, my stomach sinks. It's a guy I've seen on the news, connected to some mob guy who was accused of murdering his second in command.

I guess I'm small potatoes to a lawyer like Marcus Snyder, but I've never felt like a bigger piece of garbage. I need to get my act together. I'm better than this. And I'm going to prove it by catching this killer, even if it makes me look guilty for trying.

JANICE STILL HASN'T CALLED me back, and I'm thinking about calling her again. It's afternoon, and although this sounds like a pretty strange reaction to what's going on in my life, I went to the beach today. There's a beautiful little swimming beach called Kaimana across the park, walking distance from my house, but this morning, I couldn't remember the last time I went there and took a swim.

It's funny how that is. You can go any day, so you don't. I never got into surfing, but a lot of my friends did. But I like to be in the water. I swam to the wind sock and back, a popular workout routine in Honolulu. And then I spent a few hours lounging on the beach, which was pleasant because it was cloudy so not too hot.

For lunch, I bought a sandwich from a little shop and ate right there on the beach. People call it "dig me beach" because a lot of singles hang out there, but I wasn't looking at women. I was reflecting on the choices I've made, and the fact that I'm now keeping company with hardened criminals. And I thought about how much it would suck to be in prison, prevented from making a spontaneous decision like this, to up and go lounge on the beach.

I wonder why Janice hasn't called, and what that means.

As I'm looking at the phone, a call comes in from my attorney. He tells me he's got a window for the time of death for Lani Lum but not for Shayna McCarthy. He tells me to gather any information I have about where I was during the window, as well as a list of anyone who can corroborate my whereabouts, which brings me back to Janice.

And as we're getting off the phone he says, "Oh I have one piece of good news. Are you sure your girlfriend took those cufflinks?"

"She told me she did, but I never saw them. Why?"

"They found the cufflinks on the floor behind his dresser, so they figure he misplaced them. Don't worry about the burglary. Let's focus on clearing you for the night of the murders."

"Okay," I say.

Either Janice was messing with me, or she went back to the house and replaced the cufflinks. And if Janice was back in the house... what does that mean? The last time I saw the cufflinks they were on his dresser. Maybe she thought she took them but she dropped them? Or did we brush them off by accident, and she wanted to mess with me and make me sweat, like she did when she told me she wanted to blackmail the guy?

And as if I've summoned her spirit, I get a text:

I'm in the area. Are you home?

For a moment, I hesitate, thinking it might be better to meet up in a more public space. But how would that work, with what we have to talk about?

So I respond.

Sure. Come over. I'm home.

The idea of Janice being a serial killer is ludicrous, I tell myself. But stranger things have happened. So, I take off my shorts and put on some thick jeans, in case she tries to stab me in the leg with a lethal dose of insulin. One benefit to living in a dense area filled with low-rise condos that butt up against each other is that, since we can practically hear our neighbor rip a piece of toilet paper off its roll, there's no way she'll shoot me.

At least not here.

When Janice comes in the door, the first thing she does is hug me. Unprepared for this, I tense up. "Sorry," she says, taking a step back from me. "Old habits."

"No, no," I tell her. "It's fine. I guess I didn't expect it, after what happened last time."

"Yeah. I may have overreacted a little," she says. "Sorry."

"No major damage, but my exit was a little awkward."

She laughs, and I'm having the hardest time reading her. I wasn't expecting to talk about "us," but the conversation seems to be headed in that direction. She looks contrite, and I wonder what that means.

I offer her a beer, and she accepts. That's not her go-to beverage, but it's all I have on hand.

"Let's sit on the lanai," she says.

Shaking my head, I say, "No. We don't need our business broadcast all over the neighborhood."

It's true. Sounds ricochet around the circle like an echo chamber, something my neighbor found out the hard way when I gingerly knocked on her door and informed her that the play-by-play about how she lost her virginity that she'd been sharing with her friend was reaching a wider audience than she likely intended.

So, instead of admiring the view, we sit on my love seat, side by side, all cozy like. A regular sofa would not fit in here, but she could have sat in the lounge chair. Instead, she sat down next to me, and I wonder if that means something.

"How've you been?" she asks, placing a hand on my thigh, which is covered in denim. Thankfully, she doesn't ask why I'm wearing jeans in eighty-five-degree weather.

"Oh, you know. Person of interest in a murder. My girlfriend dumped coffee on my lap the last time I saw her. My buddy at work won't go near me because I'm radioactive and I accused him of being a murderer. Other than that, I've been great."

She looks at me, a little taken aback.

"What?" I ask. "You didn't know the cops were questioning me? I thought I told you that."

"I know. It's not that. It's just, your girlfriend? I'm sorry if I gave you the wrong impression by coming over here, but I'm not your girlfriend anymore. I thought I'd made myself clear. If that's where this is going, then maybe I should leave."

What kind of game is she playing?

I lean back on my armrest to put more space between us. "That's not why I called you over here. And you're the one who hugged me and started talking about us."

"I wasn't talking about us. I have no desire to talk about us."

"Neither do I."

"Then why did you call me and ask me over here?" she asks.

"It's about the case. Didn't you hear that Derek Anderson was shot and killed last night?"

She shrugs. "I did. Sure. But what does that have to do with me, or with us?"

My eyes widen. She's not stupid, so now I'm getting even more suspicious.

"Janice!" My hands shoot up. "We were in his house! We weren't that careful. Even with gloves, our DNA could be found there. Now that there's been a murder, they're bound to take a look at the break-in."

"What break-in?"

"Anderson filed a police report and put in an insurance claim for the diamond cufflinks you stole."

She looks at me, puzzled. "Really?"

"Yeah. Why do you find that so hard to believe?

"Because I was just messing with you. I didn't take the cuff-links." She shrugs. "Maybe one of us forgot to put them back in the right place. But how do you know that he filed a claim?"

"I hired an attorney. I told him about the break-in."

Her eyes pop open, and she sits up straight. "Did you tell him you were with me?"

"No," I lie. "But there's more. I'm the one who found Anderson last night. Well, me and this true crime podcaster named Sam Sanders."

Janice sits in stunned silence as I tell her about how I'm working together with Sam to try and solve the case. How we went there to interview Anderson. How we found the back door open and saw him, shot dead. How I ran upstairs and got photos of the shoes so I'd have a reason for my DNA being there.

"Good thinking," she says, genuinely impressed with my on-the-spot handiwork.

"But what about you?" I ask. "They could find your DNA up there, too."

"I'm not worried about it." She turns from me and holds up

her right hand, admiring her freshly manicured nails. She has great hands. Petite, with dainty fingers and skin as smooth as silk.

I find this odd, that she's not worried, because if she took the cufflinks or she didn't take the cufflinks, or if she took the cufflinks and replaced them, she has to know that her DNA is all over his house.

"Why not?" I ask

"Because I was in that house a few months ago when it was on the market, showing it to people. They'll find tons of DNA there. I'm one of many realtors who showed it. And then there's all the potential buyers who looked at it before the investor from the continent bought it. Not to mention the potential renters who looked at it, before Anderson rented the place out. Trust me, we have nothing to worry about."

She's been in the house before?

I'm completely floored.

"Why didn't you tell me?" I ask.

"Tell you what?"

"That you'd been in the house before."

"I'm sure I did. I told you I knew the house. You were probably high, or tuning me out. What's the difference?"

The difference is, this whole time, Janice has had an explanation for her DNA being in the house, and I haven't. But now that I know where we stand, I don't plan to make an issue of it.

Also, I don't tell her that I happen to know they found the cufflinks in back of his dresser. To the cops, there wasn't a break-in. They'll focus on the night of the murder. But she doesn't need to know that right now. Maybe I'll tell her at some point. I'm not even sure if I should have told her that Anderson filed an insurance claim. I don't know if I can trust her, or what I can disclose, and she seems to feel the same way.

Now it's nothing but awkward silence.

After a minute that feels like an hour, I mention that Tina is still missing.

"You seem a little obsessed with this Tina person," she says. "You talk about her a lot."

There's another pregnant pause as she picks some polish off a cuticle.

Is she jealous of Tina?

This isn't the first time she's brought her up, and my mind flashes to what Sam said about female serial killers and their motives.

"She could be the killer's third victim. Same type, with her long brown hair".

Janice rolls her eyes. "Tina has a totally different body type. She's heavier than the other two. She is not the same type at all."

Tina's full-figured, where the other two women were on the thin side. But would a serial killer care about that? Janice can be a little catty, too, so the comment doesn't surprise me.

"Sometimes I wonder, Johnny..." she says.

"You wonder what?"

"Never mind. I guess I should get going." She's only half done with her beer, not to mention her sentence.

"Don't you want to finish that thought, or your beer?"

She shakes her head. "No. I think I should go."

We stand.

She looks at me and tries to put on a friendly face, but her body language is wary. "Good luck with everything, Johnny. I wish you well."

"You too," I tell her.

In spite of the fact that she seems to think I might have something to do with the murders, and even though I have doubts about her, too, a sadness washes over me as I consider what might've been. In all probability, Janice is not a murderer, which means I'm pushing another good woman out of my life.

We hold each other's gaze as we both rise from the sofa, keeping our distance from one another.

"I can see myself out, Johnny," she says.

But before she turns and walks away, she asks, "Wait. Why did you accuse Leo of being a murderer?"

"Oh, it was stupid. He told me I'm radioactive, with the cops up my ass. So, I pushed back a little. Told him that he's the one who got Lani Lum's car."

She shrugs. "For what it's worth, Leo always gave me the creeps. The way he stared at me, the few times we met. I'd sooner believe he was a serial killer than you."

"Well, that's nice to hear. You're my alibi for the night of Lum's murder, at least part of it. Make sure to mention that to the cops if they ask."

"Right back at you," she says, raising a finger in the air as she turns around and walks away from me. I fight the urge to run and stop her.

And once again, I have to question if Leo was lying when he said that he didn't notice Lani Lum. Leo likes to look at women, even if he has an attitude about them, especially the good-looking ones.

The little wiggle in her walk as Janice makes her way to my front door still gives me a charge. And as I get a glimpse of her manicured hand as she blows me a kiss goodbye, I take a deep breath and try to focus on the silver lining. I am now free to meet up with Linda Chun, a woman who I'm almost certain is not a murderer, which is more than I can say for Janice.

It's not much of a silver lining, but for now, it's all I've got.

TWENTY-FIVE

JOHNNY

We're at Sam's vacation rental in Kailua, and he's practically salivating over the recordings he got when he visited with Tina's Auntie Marjorie on Kaua'i, who happened to be a medium, eager to show off her skills. She lives in a small plantation-style house in Kapa'a, on the east side of the island.

The bottom line is, Auntie Marjorie has not heard from Tina, and she's very concerned about her niece. She confirmed that her niece has no relatives in California that she knows of. But still, Sam was able to score some podcast-worthy material for the show.

I listen as Sam plays a segment for me. Meditation music twinkles magically in the background. Marjorie tells Sam she needs to connect with "the frequency" and starts to hum.

Ommmmmm.

Ommmmmm.

Ommmmmm.

We hear her breath rise and fall as she searches for a connection to the spirit world. I wish we had visuals, and I tell this to Sam. He says he will describe the scene for the listeners before he gets to her clip:

A late middle-aged woman sits before me, dressed in a paisley caftan, her auburn hair up in a bun, her eyes shut tight, her weathered brow furrowed in deep concentration. A candle flickers on the table between us.

He flashes me a cheeky grin.

Sam is good at this. I'll give him that.

Finally, she speaks.

It's Tina.

I see her.

Sam tells me that Marjorie, at this point, grabbed his arm and dug her nails into his flesh.

She's alive.

But time is running out.

Kimo. It's Kimo.

She's trembling.

He's seething with rage.

He wants to kill her.

He wants to kill Tina.

Sam stops the recording. "You get the drift."

"You believe any of this garbage?"

"No. Of course not. She's a loon. Or a charlatan, looking for some free publicity. She pedals her wares to tourists, out of a shop in Hanalei. She was practically salivating at the chance to get on my channel. But she did corroborate what you told me about the ex being violent. I think we may be looking at two different crimes," Sam says. "I don't think Tina's connected to the other two murders. My money's on the violent husband for her disappearance. Kimo Fernandez. I think he did something to her."

"You mean the violent *ex*-husband. Tina's divorced."

"No," Sam says. "They've been separated for over a year,

according to Marjorie. But they're still fighting over money, so they haven't finalized it yet. A very bitter divorce, from what she told me. Tina has some family money she inherited a while back. No prenup. So Kimo would get it all if she died. She has no other relatives, except Marjorie. And anyway, a spouse comes first."

I recount my experience with Kimo Fernandez and how he got in my face at the Royal, when he was looking for Tina. The bruises we saw on her arm. And then something dawns on me.

"Don't male serial killers sometimes go after proxies? Women who look like women they're angry with?"

"They do. But I still think it's a woman," Sam says. "I don't think Tina's disappearance is connected to the other two murders."

"Yeah. So you said. But we can't get tunnel vision, Sam. That's what happened with the cops, right? Dana Ireland? The Honolulu Strangler? They get fixated on a suspect and try to fit the evidence to the theory instead of the other way around. We need to be better than that."

So, he considers my idea and agrees with me that Kimo Fernandez merits further investigation. Even if he's not our serial killer, he very well may have killed Tina or kidnapped her, and Sam agrees to look into it more and see if he had access to insulin.

And then another thought occurs to me.

"If they're still married, if Tina dies, Kimo Fernandez gets everything. Maybe even a life insurance payout. Did you check on that? See if he increased it lately?"

"I can. And yeah. Classic motive for killing a spouse. But he'd be the first suspect," Sam points out. "And what about the other women? What would be the motive for killing them?"

I shrug. "Maybe it's a ruse. Make it look like a serial killer, to get Tina out of the way and get the money."

"I don't know, Johnny. That sounds like a stretch. He'd have to be a total psychopath."

"Or a man who really wants her money. It would also explain the method. Maybe he couldn't stomach a more hands-on approach. Maybe it's a man who's not serial killer material."

Sam blows out a breath. "So we'd be looking for someone who's more of the contract killer personality profile."

"If you say so."

"Anyway, with this and the Anderson recordings, I've almost got enough for an episode. I'll run down info on this Fernandez guy. Then we can sit down and piece it together. I've got a business to run, and I need to upload by Monday afternoon. I have deadlines. Sponsors."

Today is Friday. I work both weekend days. I tell him this, and we agree to meet Monday morning to finalize the episode. Then I tell Sam I need to go.

I'M MEETING with Uncle Mel for a late breakfast at Pat's Place, an iconic greasy spoon that's been raking in a fortune in Honolulu for over half a century. Mel's favorite spot, aside from the Honu Club. I walk in and see him back-slapping the manager.

"This guy," Mel says to me, gripping him by the arm. "Like a bruddha to me."

"Hey," I say, greeting the manager with a head nod. He's short and stout with a weathered face and a bro vibe.

"You know my nephew, Johnny?" Mel says.

We don't know each other. Mel knows this, but it's part of the ritual. It's a mob scene and there's an hour or more wait, but Mel and I are soon ferried to a choice table in the corner, although we don't have a reservation. I tried but they were full. This was kind of a last-minute decision.

Mel presses a bill in the manager's palm as he seats us, no idea how much. I feel kind of bad about this, since this was my idea. I could learn a thing or two from Uncle Mel.

After we order, we get down to business. Mel tells me that it was, indeed, an insulin overdose for both of the victims. HPD plans to make a statement to that effect today or tomorrow. I fill him in on my meeting with Marcus Snyder and thank him for paying the retainer. Then I tell him I pretty much have an alibi for the night of Lani Lum's murder.

"Pretty much?"

"Yeah. They say she died between two a.m. and two p.m. on May twelfth. I was at my girl's house from around six that night to six in the morning. Then I drove home. I stopped at Starbucks on Kapahulu on my way, at around seven. Then I was home until I arrived for my shift around eleven."

"So, you've got four hours unaccounted for?"

"Yeah. But my attorney thinks it's not a big problem. He says the fact that they can't get a tight window is going to make it hard to prosecute the case. I guess that's good."

"Good? Two women are dead. There's a serial killer who might strike again. I don't see how any of this is good. And now you're going off doing this podcast, trying to profit off of it. I don't like it, Johnny. It's a bad look."

"It's not like that," I tell Mel.

Then I give him a recap of everything we've discovered so far. What our fears are about Tina. Her husband. The financial motivations he might have for getting rid of her.

The waitress slaps down our plates full of food, and Mel digs in. Me, I've sort of lost my appetite. I want Mel to be proud of me, and he's anything but. And when I tell him about my theory that Tina's husband could've done the other murders as a ruse, he stops eating and rests his head on his fingertips. Then he shakes his head from side to side. Then he lets out a long sigh.

Without a word, he picks up his fork and continues to eat his breakfast.

After a few minutes of picking at my meal, my mouth starts to water from the savory scents of bacon, butter, and browning batter. I start to wolf it down, catching up to Mel as we engage in small talk, but tension lingers underneath the banter.

Mel asks me about Janice, and I tell him that we broke up, but that she'll alibi for the night of the murder. He gives me the scoop on his wife of forty years, Auntie Mia, who has started teaching tai chi to senior citizens and loves it. And just when I think he's done scolding me for what he perceives to be my greed or naïveté or both, he says something that gets my attention.

"You know that sometimes killers like to insert themselves in the investigation, right?"

"Yeah," I say. "We talked about this. You can't possibly think—"

"Not you, numb nuts."

"Then who? Janice?"

Mel rolls his eyes. "The podcaster. Did you know that he arrived on the island a week before the first murder?"

My eyes widen. "I did not know that. I thought he came to cover the murders."

"Did he tell you that?"

"No. I assumed. So either it's a complete coincidence that he was here a week before the first murder..."

"Or he had a reason to believe there would be a story," Mel says.

"I don't believe in coincidences."

"Me either, Johnny. Watch your back with that guy."

I'm not letting this stop me from putting out that podcast episode. It was my idea, and what would Sam have to gain from killing me if his motive is getting a good story? Plus, he may have a reason for being here a week before the first murder.

But something strikes me, as I think back on the other two murders. If Tina's disappearance is connected, why wouldn't he have dumped the body by now and taken credit?

Which brings me back to the point of the episode, and my original question:

Where's Tina?

TWENTY-SIX
TINA

Tina Fernandez looks at her face in the mirror and cringes.

The bruise is a swirl of purple, black, and green. The swelling is probably at its peak, and she'd rather not be seen in public like this. But it's not like she has much choice.

She dabs her concealer on the contusion, a little at a time. Because it hurts a lot, and also because it can't look too obvious, and if she puts too much on, it will appear caked and call attention to her. She had it looking good before she boarded the plane, but now some of the makeup has sweated off her face. They got stuck on the tarmac for a while, and it was stiflingly hot. She almost had a panic attack, but managed to hold it together.

So far, there's been nothing on the news about her being a missing person. But people will figure out sooner or later that she has no relatives in California, and by then, she will need to be somewhere else. Somewhere she can't be found until she wants to be found.

She looks at her wrists, still raw from the rope burns, and

pulls her cardigan over the telltale marks. They will scar, for sure.

She could play this another way, but every bone in her body is telling her to disappear. Now. Before it's too late. When the time is right, she can return.

But that time is not now.

Now, she has to regroup.

Lie low.

Figure out her next steps.

So, she leaves the airport bathroom and makes her way to the taxi stand, where she can pay in cash. When she gets to her destination, she'll figure out the rest.

For now, she's safe.

And that's all that matters.

TWENTY-SEVEN
JOHNNY

The little cottage Sam rents is walking distance to Kailua Beach, probably the most beautiful stretch of white sand beach in the world. Powdery white and fine, it insinuates itself into shoes and towels and beach toys, gets stuck in your hair and inside your ears when you body surf or boogie board, but it's totally worth it.

I remember Mom complaining about it when I was little, that she could never get the Kailua sand out of her car when we came here. Still, we came often. She'd take off for long power walks down the beach a few miles to the other end, grab a coffee at the little shop, and stroll back. Dad and I built sand castles or roughhoused in the water.

It's safe, with a sandy bottom and not too rough. Great for kids. The only problem is the Portuguese man o' wars, bright purple jellyfish with footlong tails that can wrap around an arm or leg. They are abundant, and they sting like hell. Mom always came prepared with meat tenderizer, which she used on me on more than a few occasions. I'm not sure if it helped, but I think it made her feel better to take some action.

Before the Obamas made it a tourist attraction, Kailua Beach was more of a local best-kept secret, but now it's inundated with locals and tourists. I had to park blocks away, but it was a nice walk. When I arrive at his place, I decide to ask Sam straight out about the timing of his arrival in the islands. Give him a chance to explain himself.

"I thought I told you," Sam says. "I came to do a story on the Honolulu Strangler. Poke the bear a little. See if I could get some interest in reviving it. They've got a cold case unit now in Honolulu. I thought they might be getting close to closing it, with the new technology they have. Breaking that story would be epic. But then a dead body showed up, and I got sidetracked. Plus, it's easier here than in Seattle to do podcasting. It's not a two-party state, so I can record anything I want without even telling anyone I'm doing it."

It seems like a good explanation, but it's still a weird coincidence about the timing. I actually did some research to see if there have been any cases of a true crime podcaster being the killer in a case they were investigating. And there have not been.

But there have been numerous instances of amateur detectives inserting themselves into investigations and becoming suspects, or worse. The Green River Killer, found guilty of the murders. The Honolulu Strangler, still a suspect even in death. Never charged. Never cleared.

Maybe that will be me if we don't find out who did these murders. If the case goes cold. The guy who the police couldn't charge, with a cloud of doubt hanging over my head for the rest of my life. Mel might be right. Keeping a low profile and letting this blow over. That's the safe thing to do.

But of course, that's not what I'm doing. I'm here with Sam, and we're putting together what could be the best episode he's ever done. Because guess what? Kimo Fernandez took a vacation. He's in New Zealand on a two-week adventure, hiking off the grid, according to his workplace. He left the day Tina didn't show up for work. We plan to end with that.

Sam starts with an overview of the facts, then I get a chance to tell my side of the story. He asks me to explain how I got involved in the case. I tell him that I work at the Royal. How I noticed Lani Lum, talking to Derek Anderson, but that I'd never laid eyes on Shayna McCarthy. How I saw Anderson chatting up Tina before she disappeared. How he got on my radar as a potential suspect.

We move on to the night we found Derek Anderson, and Sam gives listeners a visceral description of the scene. Blood everywhere. The stench. The insects feeding on him, that I'm pretty sure he didn't stay around long enough to see, but it makes for good, if somewhat nauseating, storytelling. The body, positioned in a recliner. The hit, execution-style.

Auntie Marjorie injects some comic relief, but then I reiterate the fact that Tina came to work with bruises on her arm. That her husband stalked her at work. Sam mentions that we're trying to track down her husband, but that he's conveniently taken a vacation.

Then he says something that changes everything, springing it on me as we're recording.

"Turns out, Shayna McCarthy has a connection to Kimo Fernandez."

"Whoa! What the f... Dude! Why didn't you tell me that before?"

"I'm telling you now."

"On the air!?"

Sam chuckles. "You should see the look on your face, man."

And I have to hand it to him. This is good stuff. I couldn't have faked that kind of incredulity. "Okay. *And...*"

"They used to be an item. Before he married Tina."

"Holy shit. Am I allowed to say that on the air?"

"Yeah, doofus. You're allowed to say that on the air. This isn't Sesame Street."

"What do you think it means?"

"I think it means, maybe we should title this episode, *Where's Kimo?* Cause if we find Kimo, we might find Tina."

"But here's the thing," I say. "If Tina's connected to the other murders, why hasn't the killer dumped the body and taken credit? And how does Derek Anderson's murder play into this? That seemed more like a mob hit than a serial killer murder."

"I guess we have more investigating to do."

He says some closing words, and we're out.

"Nice work. Just like I thought. You're a natural."

"So what do we do now?"

"I'll edit it all together and upload this afternoon."

"No, I mean, what do we do to move the case forward?"

Sam shrugs. "I'm not a detective."

"Don't you want to solve the case?"

"Sure. But that's not why I'm here. I'm here to break a story. Keep an eye on the case. Keep the cops from getting tunnel vision. We don't have the resources or the know-how to solve the case."

Sam has a point, but still.

I want to solve the case, so I let him do his thing, and I go do research on someone who might be useful to me. Shayna McCarthy's jilted fiancé, who's still, as far as I know, a person of interest in her murder.

SHAYNA MCCARTHY'S fiancé turned out to be an accountant named Greg Masters, who works at a large firm in downtown Honolulu. I left him a message, letting him know about our upcoming podcast episode and that he might want to tune in. Once the news breaks about Kimo Fernandez and his connection to Shayna McCarthy, I'm sure he'll be dying to talk to us. This could make a good follow-up to our first episode, but I don't say anything to Sam yet.

Meanwhile, I try to nail down a date with Linda Chun, who arrives tomorrow for a quick three-day stay. Something to do with her paternal grandmother's estate. That sounds like a rich person's problem, but she assures me it's just a figure of speech. Her grandmother didn't have much, but what she had needed to be handled, and Linda was the only one who could do it.

I work the next five days in a row, from midday to evening, so my availability is limited to mornings, which is not exactly prime dating time. But maybe that's okay. Maybe this isn't a date. Just two old friends getting together. I don't need that kind of complication right now anyway.

I haven't heard a word from Janice, and I guess that shouldn't surprise me.

Linda and I settle on the day after tomorrow, which is Wednesday. I make a reservation at a nice place on Kaimana Beach, at the Kaimana Beach Hotel.

Then I roll a joint.

Yeah. I know. I was supposed to cut out the weed.

But I've cut back. *A lot.*

And I enjoy the ritual of smoking a joint. I like separating the seeds. I like smelling the weed. I like the way it crunches under my finger when I roll it in the paper. I like to take a long, lingering whiff before I light it, savoring it in anticipation. I even enjoy the burning sensation in my lungs.

So, I do all of this, but I only let myself take a few hits before I go and flush it down the toilet.

Baby steps.
And then I listen to our podcast.

TWENTY-EIGHT
JOHNNY

Ten hours later, I'm at work, and the vibe towards me at the Royal is a one-eighty from the last time I was here. The podcast hasn't even been up a day, but so far, it's surpassing any of Sam's past episodes in terms of views and likes and comments, by nearly double. Instead of a pariah, I'm a minor celebrity, and one who has come to the aid of one of our own.

Mandy is working the valet desk today, still covering for Tina.

"Gosh, Johnny," she says, placing a hand on my forearm. "Nice going. I hope they find Tina. Maybe now the cops will take it more seriously, with all the pressure you put on them with your show." Her sudden concern for Tina seems disingenuous.

The last thing I want to do right now is irritate the cops, so my stomach twists a little as I think about how this might play out with them. Still, I'm cleared for the night of Lani Lum's murder. They've also cleared Shayna McCarthy's fiancé for her murder. Derek Anderson is obviously in the clear. And now they've got nothing. So, at least I gave them someone to chew on: Kimo Fernandez.

Maybe they'll thank me.

Yeah, right.

I'm not on duty yet, so I head downstairs to where the conference rooms are to grab a cup of coffee. It's supposed to be for the guests, but nobody says anything if we help ourselves. I do it often, and so does everyone else.

After I pour myself a cup, I head over to where I hang out on breaks, sit down, and think back on the day someone saw me here with Shayna McCarthy. Well, not with her. But in the same vicinity as her. Because whoever claims to have seen me could be trying to frame me or deflect attention from themselves. Whoever told the cops or management that they saw me down here at the same time as Shayna McCarthy could have been the person who murdered her.

I think about Kimo Fernandez, and the fact that he used to date her. That can't be a coincidence. He doesn't like me. He got in my face that day. Maybe he saw this is an opportunity to get back at me. But that doesn't make sense because why would anyone believe him? Why would they even let him hang out down here? He was escorted off the property by security, so it probably wasn't him.

The obvious choice of course is Leo. He's off today, so it'll be interesting to see if the halo effect I'm getting from the podcast will extend to him. I doubt it. He's not the type to be impressed by something like that. More than likely, I've made an enemy out of him. He could be the one who said he saw me here. And maybe he did. It's quite possible she was down here when I was down here, and that nobody is lying or trying to set me up.

And finally, there's Janice. Could she have been here checking up on me? But if it's a jealousy thing, that wouldn't make any sense. She could've seen me staring at Lani Lum and gotten her panties in a knot, but I've never laid eyes on Shayna McCarthy, so Janice would have no reason to feel jealous of her. I'm obviously missing something.

So, I close my eyes and quiet my mind, trying to see if I can remember something. Anything, from that day. Something is at the edge of my consciousness, but I can't quite reach it. But then my phone buzzes, snapping me out of my stupor.

Maybe I should try hypnosis.

It's Sam, and I pick up, expecting him to start in on how great the episode was.

But that's not what he says.

"Seems there's more to Derek Anderson than we thought," he says.

"What do you mean?"

"His ex-girlfriend heard our podcast and contacted me. And what she said will blow your mind. Look, I can't go into it now. I have to run. But call me later, when you get off work. We need to talk. Soon."

"Wait a minute," I yell into the phone.

But he's gone.

Seriously?

He's going to leave me hanging like this?

And then I remember the first person I thought of when Detective Akana said they saw me near Shayna McCarthy on her bachelorette weekend. I thought of Derek Anderson and the fact that he didn't like me. That he might have been the one to say he saw me sitting near her.

Jumping out of my chair, I realize I'm a few minutes late, so I bound up the stairs to the valet desk.

Upon my late arrival, Mandy shoots me a sideways glance. "Don't let it go to your head, Johnny," she says. "You still have to do your job."

Then she hands me a set of keys and sends me to park a Mercedes SUV.

IT'S ALMOST nine o'clock in the evening when I get off work and call Sam, but I get his voicemail. Tomorrow morning, I'm meeting Linda Chun for breakfast. I think about canceling so I can catch up with him and find out what the hell is going on.

Why isn't he picking up?

I'm about five minutes into my fifteen-minute drive home when he calls. He's babbling on in a stream-of-consciousness fashion, and his phone is cutting in and out, so I'm only getting pieces of what he's saying.

"Sam," I say. "Calm down. Talk to me nice and calm, like you do on your podcast."

I hear him take a breath, and then he says, "I'm not sure what this means. But according to Anderson's ex-girlfriend, the guy was kind of a freak."

I try not to let myself feel vindicated that there was something off about the guy as I listen to what Sam is telling me. I've used up a lot of my nine lives regarding this case, and I don't need any bad mana coming my way by getting all full of myself.

He tells me that his girlfriend broke it off with him the last time she was in Honolulu. Apparently, those were her shoes and makeup at his house. It turns out he was hooking up with a lot of different women, and she called him out on it. He turned it around on the girlfriend. Blamed it all on her for being too vanilla.

She didn't want to get too into the weeds about the details, but she told Sam the handle he used on a couple of freaky websites and told him to verify that what she was saying was true. He was the kind of guy who liked to have his cake and eat it too, she said. Have a respectable woman on his arm at functions and get his kicks on the side. He was also on some cheater website that married people use for sexual side gigs.

Sam says she told the police all of this, and she thinks a jealous husband could've been the one to kill him. She didn't seem too broken up about it, either. She wants us to out him about it on our podcast, although she declined to be interviewed for the next episode and wants to remain anonymous. Maybe she's the one who killed him. She certainly sounds pissed off enough to have done it.

After we hang up, my mind reels with the implications.

Just because he was a sex freak it doesn't mean he's a serial killer, but it certainly makes it seem more plausible. A jealous husband makes sense, especially if he went after the wrong man's woman—or the wrong woman.

TWENTY-NINE
JOHNNY

The first thing I notice about my old girlfriend Linda Chun is that she's assimilated to the SoCal lifestyle. If I didn't know better, I'd never peg her for a local public high school grad. She looks like the type of woman who gets facials and Botox and spa treatments, even if she doesn't need them.

I lived in LA. I know the drill there. It's what women do, especially the ones with money, so I'm not blaming her for caving to peer pressure. She also has a bust that's a few sizes larger than I remember.

Don't get me wrong. I'm not complaining. She's a total knockout. I sort of did a double-take when I saw her in the lobby, looking so much different from the fresh-faced and inno-cent schoolgirl that I remember, wearing a white linen dress that hugged what's left of her curves and spiky-heeled sandals that seemed out of place mid-morning in Honolulu.

Still, after a bit of chit-chat, the Linda I know starts to break through. Her California girl lilt gives way to a slight local accent, and the veneer of confidence breaks down as she twirls her dark, silky hair in her fingers, like she used to when we were young. A flash of memory hits me. I liked running my fingers through her hair. It always smelled like mangos.

We're at an open-air restaurant on Kaimana Beach, the Hau Tree Lanai, facing the ocean, on a veranda that sports a tree through its center. The same tree where, reportedly, Robert Louis Stevenson sat and wrote and relaxed during his time in Honolulu. There's a lot of history here at this spot. History of the islands. History of me.

Linda and I haven't talked about her husband's death at all. She has no kids, but she was a stepmother to his two children, a boy and a girl, now grown. I don't know if she keeps in touch with them. It seems like a sensitive subject, so I don't bring it up.

Instead, she listens patiently as I tell her all about the insanity that is my life right now. Linda's still a great listener. I always loved that about her. The way she gives you her full, undivided attention, like you're the most important person in the world. I explain how my last relationship fell apart, and run Janice's "grass is greener" theory by her.

She puts a hand on mine. "Johnny. That's bullshit."

I chuckle. Linda hardly ever swears, and it seems odd, coming out of her virginal ruby lips. "You didn't come from money," she says. "Not like my late husband. You did the best you could. It's not that easy to make it if you start out with nothing. It's not your fault your mom got sick and you couldn't go away to college. At least you're trying. And that podcast of yours was fantastic. I think you may be on to something. You're not a dreamer, you're a go-getter. I always admired that about you, even if you left me behind in your pursuits."

There's an awkward silence as I struggle to form a response.

"Thanks," I say. "And I'm sorry."

"Oh, not at all. That's not what I meant. It turned out fine for me," she says. "I'm right where I want to be. This town is too small for my taste. Too constricting. I've built a life for myself where I am. I'm happy."

I nod, wondering if I should say something about my desire to move away, but something holds me back. "So, you're working as a nurse?"

She takes a bite of her salad and nods. After she finishes, she says, "Yes. I don't need the money. But I like working. It gives me a sense of purpose, and great health insurance. My husband never wanted me to work. He thought it would make him look bad, like he couldn't provide for me. But I insisted."

I'm starting to get the feeling that Linda's marriage wasn't so great, which could be why she never talks about him. Or else I'm reading too much into it.

But then she says, "I don't mean to be critical of Rob. He was a great provider, and that's what I wanted at the time. He spoiled me. Allowed me to go to college and pursue my dream of being a nurse. At first, I loved the attention and the security, after how I grew up. I didn't want to feel like a charity case, you know?"

"Why would you feel like a charity case?"

"His first wife came from money, like him. And I always felt that his friends and business associates were judging me, like I was some kind of gold digger. But at work, I was just me. A nurse, good at my job. I needed that validation."

"I get that," I say. "It's commendable."

And I start to remember something about Linda. Something that pushed me away the first time. She's almost too good. Like saintly good. And saintly good isn't very hot.

But I suppress that thought, and remind myself that Janice convinced me to start ripping off my customers, she stalked me at work, and she might even be a murderer, although I doubt that. Still, maybe a saint of a woman is exactly what I need right now, so I try to enjoy my lunch with Linda, and push down the nagging feeling in my gut that perhaps Linda Chun is better left in my past.

After I finish my lunch with Linda, I head straight to work. I've been holding back on talking to Sam for a couple of reasons. First, the timing of his arrival in the islands. There hasn't been a case of a podcaster being behind a murder they were investigating, but that doesn't mean it couldn't happen. And, I'm not sure how much I can trust Sam or how much I want to divulge about what I'm thinking may have happened to Derek Anderson.

I did some more research on Sam. He comes from a wealthy family, which is probably why he can fly all over the country and do these podcast episodes. I'm sure he has a trust fund. It's that kind of family. And something a little strange happened his sophomore year of college, at a small private school in Oregon. There were a series of sexual assaults on campus that year. Three women were attacked and groped. All of them managed to escape the attacker. None of them saw the guy's face clearly enough to identify a suspect.

Nobody was ever charged, but Sam changed schools the next year. He transferred from a lower-tier school to a more prestigious university, which isn't unheard of. Still, it stuck out to me. His parents have the kind of money that could help cover something like that up. Innocent until proven guilty, I remind myself. But I haven't crossed him off my list.

Sam, who keeps insisting the killer is a woman.

Leo gives me a hard stare as I approach the valet desk. "Here he is. The man of the hour."

"What is your problem?" I say to him.

"You're my problem," he says. "But not for long."

My lips press into a tight grimace. "What's that supposed to mean? Are you threatening me?"

"No, dumb ass. I mean my shift is ending soon." He slips into a silver Infiniti sedan and goes on his way.

Leo works the early shift today, which means we're only doubled up for about an hour, during the lunch rush. I wonder, though, if his message was something more. Leo's reaction seems a bit over the top to me, and I think again about the three elements in a suspect the cops always look for: means, motive, and opportunity.

Of all the people close to this case, I have to admit, Leo looks pretty good for it, with his access to insulin and the fact that he works here and could have interacted with the victims. The motive is somewhat weak, based solely on some outdated attitudes towards women. But that's only what he says out loud. Who knows what he's actually thinking?

He could have looked in Lani Lum's glovebox and found her address, or Shayna McCarthy's for that matter. I don't know if he's the one who parked Shayna's car, or if she even had a car here at all. Or if she has a glovebox that locks or doesn't lock. But he used to work the front desk, so he knows how to look up her record, which would have her address and phone number. Plus, it's not that hard to find someone's address these days. It only takes a quick search.

Leo has something on me, sort of, so I need to be careful. Otherwise, I might do more digging. Talk to some of the employees. But I can't. If he tells the cops I was looking in Derek Anderson's file, that won't be good, especially now that he's been murdered.

And as I'm about to grab a white Subaru Outback and whisk it into the parking garage, I see a cop car drive up. The lights aren't flashing, but still, my stomach sinks. A scene flashes through my mind where I hop in the Subaru and take off like Harrison Ford, looking for the one-armed man, racing off into hiding until I can prove my innocence. But that's only in the cop shows, and in a city where you can cross over into another state. Fleeing on an island is not the wisest course of action. There's no place to run, and maybe one or two degrees of separation between two total strangers.

So instead of adding grand theft auto to my rap sheet, I hop in the vehicle and drive it calmly toward the parking garage, doing my job. I have no reason to think they're here to talk to me in particular, and if I stop, I'll look even more guilty.

But of course, panic starts to hit me, and soon the floodgates will open, exposing my trespasses and my secrets. And once again, I feel like coming clean about the break-in might be my best bet. At least if I did that, I'd have nothing to hide regarding Derek Anderson and maybe they'll believe me that I had nothing to do with these murders.

Taking my time, I drive the car up an extra floor, pull out my phone, and leave a message for Marcus Snyder, telling my attorney that the cops are at the Royal, but I have no idea why yet, and letting him know to be on standby.

And that turns out to be a good move when I exit the garage and see Officer Yoshimura strolling my way. "We'd like to have a chat with you," he says.

It's only a chat, I tell myself. But I know what that means.

"I just started my shift. Can it wait?"

Yoshimura shakes his head. "Arrangements have been made. Please, come with me."

Arrangements?

And now my vision starts to narrow. A vice clamps my temples. My pulse pounds in my ears and for a minute, I forget how to breathe.

Am I having a stroke?

Or a heart attack?

Then I suck air into my lungs like a drowning man pulled from the sea. Puddles form in my pits and palms as I process what's happening.

Because Officer Yoshimura gestured towards the cop car, and that's where we're headed. We're not staying here at the hotel to talk. He's taking me down to the station.

"Am I under arrest?" I ask.

But he doesn't answer me.

"Let's go," he says, taking me by the arm.

"Can I call my attorney?"

"You have that right," he says.

And I do.

THIRTY-ONE
JOHNNY

I've never thought of myself as claustrophobic, but between the ride over here, knowing that I couldn't open the car door if I wanted to, and the fact that I've been sitting in the small room by myself for over thirty minutes, I'm starting to feel a little panicky. Maybe everybody is claustrophobic under the right circumstances. They didn't cuff me, though, or read me my rights. I could have refused to come, but I didn't want to make a scene at work.

As I start to stress myself into a panic attack thinking about how long they might leave me sitting here and what I would do if I needed to use the bathroom, the door opens and Marcus Snyder walks in.

Never in my life have I been so happy to see a person I barely know.

"What's going on?" I ask him.

He looks me up and down. I'm sweating bullets, and they are dripping down my face

"You look guilty as fuck," he says. "You're not, right? I need to know what I'm dealing with here."

"I didn't kill Derek Anderson, if that's what you mean."

"Are you seriously sweating like a stuck pig for a stupid break-in where you didn't even take anything?"

I actually think my lawyer's more disgusted with me for being a wuss than he would be if I'd confessed to murder. I guess that's what a job like his does to a person. You lose your humanity. Or maybe he never had it to begin with. Maybe that's the kind of person who makes for an effective defense attorney. Right now, I'm glad he's on my side. I would not want this guy as my enemy.

"Why am I here?" I ask.

"They found your DNA up in Derek Anderson's bedroom. And they also have a neighbor who claims he saw your car parked across the street a few nights before his murder. Do you have an explanation for this?"

My jaw drops. "I didn't give them my DNA. How in the hell do they have my DNA?"

"Not a big fan of true crime? Anything you discard these days. A tissue. A coffee cup. A cigarette butt. They can grab it and test it without a warrant. Perfectly legal."

I think about the coffee I drink at the Royal, and wonder if the cops were watching me there. I also think about Leo and wonder if he's trying to set me up.

"Can you find out what they tested?"

Snyder shakes his head no. "They haven't arrested you yet, so no. And that's not important. Do you have an explanation for your DNA being in Anderson's bedroom, aside from the fact that you broke into his house?"

"Yeah," I say. "I ran up there and took some photos for the podcast, like the women's shoes in the closet, to prove he's the serial killer."

"That's not a very good explanation."

"Why?" I ask.

"Because how would you know that there were women's shoes in his closet if you hadn't been there before?"

"I'll tell them I went up to poke around a little. Get stuff for the podcast. And then I found the shoes."

"Were you sitting across from his house a few days before the murder?"

"Yeah. I was. I was thinking about breaking in again and taking photos of the shoes, then sending them anonymously to the police. I thought he was the killer. And by the way, we found out some pretty freaky stuff about him from his old girlfriend. Maybe he is a serial killer."

My attorney is getting frustrated with me, and I've only been here a few minutes. "Can we please focus on you and forget about this serial killer bullshit? You're not here for those murders. What explanation are you going to give the cops to explain why you were stalking Derek Anderson that doesn't make you stream sweat like a human pasta strainer?"

"I was watching the house, not stalking him. I thought he was guilty. And I wasn't the only one. Sam Snyder, that podcaster, was there that night, watching me watch the house. That's how we met."

"That's the first useful piece of information you've given me," Snyder says.

"How so?"

My lawyer smirks. "All you need for reasonable doubt is another plausible suspect. Was the interview with Anderson his idea or yours?"

"The podcast was my idea but the interview was his."

"Excellent. Keep your mouth shut and answer only when I tell you to. Got it?"

I nod.

He goes over to the door and knocks on it.

The door opens. Officer Yoshimura and Detective Akana

step into the room and sit across the table from me. My attorney sits next to me.

Akana is younger than Yoshimura by about a decade, with a commanding presence that causes me to sit up straighter in my chair. This is a woman who has ambitions. The kind of woman who wants to close a high-profile case, and close it fast. She repeats what my attorney said about what they have on me, and asks if I have anything to say.

I turn to Snyder and shrug.

"Do you have an actual question for my client?" he says.

What she asks catches me by surprise. "Did you steal cufflinks from Derek Anderson's house and then throw them behind his dresser the night of the murder?"

"I did not," I reply, thinking about how lucky I am that she asked me that precise question. But then my mind flashes again to Leo. Why would she even go there, unless he said something about me looking in his file?

"Why were you in his room?"

I tell her what I rehearsed, and since it's the truth, it goes well.

She lobs me another soft ball. "Why were you stalking Derek Anderson?"

"I wasn't stalking him."

"We hear you're a little obsessed with him."

Narrowing my eyes on her, I push back a little. "I'm just a concerned citizen, trying to get a killer off the streets."

Detective Akana leans in, getting in my face, trying to get me to back down. "You think Derek Anderson is a killer? Derek Anderson, who was shot dead?"

"Talk to Anderson's girlfriend. She'll tell you what a freak he was. Lots of people could've wanted him dead. And he still could've been the person who killed those two women. Have you noticed that the killings stopped, now that he's out of the picture?"

I catch my attorney's eye, and damn if he doesn't look a little bit impressed with me.

But his admiration is short-lived.

"So, you fancy yourself a vigilante?" Detective Akana says.

"Don't answer that," Snyder barks.

"Your client has a pattern," Detective Akana says. "And a temper. He was in a bar fight five years ago, defending a woman's honor. It went to court. And then—"

"Yeah, as the plaintiff, not the defendant. And the case was dismissed after my client dropped the charges. And that's completely irrelevant to the matter of Derek Anderson's murder, so stop trying to spin this narrative to fit your insane theory. We're leaving."

"Not so fast. As I was going to say," Akana's gaze flicks to me and back to my attorney, "the guy from the bar fight is dead now, so we can't even get his side of the story. Pretty convenient for your client. Died in a tragic fall," she says.

"That's none of our concern. You've got nothing, and you know it. Maybe you should try writing fiction. We're leaving."

With that, Snyder bolts up and pushes his chair back so hard that it nearly topples over.

Before I can stop the words from coming out of my mouth, they float out of my lips and over the table top towards my inquisitor. "I'll take a lie detector test," I say. "I want to clear myself. I had nothing to do with Derek Anderson's murder, and I want the world to know it."

Snyder shoots daggers at me. I know I'm going to catch hell for this, but I think it's the right move. I didn't kill Anderson, and it's better they think I have nothing to hide. Still, it could backfire. I do have secrets, so I hold my breath as she ponders my offer, hoping I didn't just screw myself to the wall. Hoping that she doesn't take me up on it.

"That won't be necessary at this time," Denise Akana says.

I let out a long breath and try not to smile.

WHEN WE GET to the parking lot and reach Snyder's car, I'm expecting my attorney to give me a lift, so I go for the passenger seat door handle.

"What the hell are you doing?" he asks.

"I need a ride. My car's back at the Royal."

"Do I look like an Uber driver to you? And if you ever do anything that stupid again, I'm going to fire you as a client and keep the retainer." With that, he gets in his car and drives away.

I open a ride share app on my phone and vow that next time, if there is a next time, I'll try harder to quit while I'm ahead and keep my big mouth shut.

Then I notice a text message from Greg Masters, Shayna McCarthy's ex-fiancé.

I have information for you about Kimo Fernandez. Call me. Soon.

THIRTY-TWO

JOHNNY

When I arrive at the Royal, I duck into the garage to grab my car, not bothering to check if they need me. After all, they made "arrangements." Which means that everyone knows I'm a suspect in a murder investigation.

Again.

I'm not ready to face anyone here.

But as luck would have it, I run smack into Leo as I'm running up the staircase to get my car. He tries to ignore me, but I grab him by the shoulder and spin him around.

"Did you say something to the cops about me?" I ask.

His face flushes with anger. "Get your hands off me," he says. "Or I'll call security."

Backing away from him and relaxing my posture, I say, "Don't be so dramatic, Leo. What did you tell them?"

Leo scoffs. "I know you've been up to something for the past year or so. I got a sixth sense about this stuff. Whatever you've gotten yourself into, it's on you, Johnny."

"I'm not a freaking murderer, and you know it."

"And I'm not going to lie to the cops for you."

"I didn't do anything," I say.

But my delivery is weak. I did do something. I ripped off a few of our customers. And even if Leo doesn't have any proof of that, he could make things very difficult for me if he decides to mention it to the cops

But I can't focus on that right now. Right now, I have to clear myself of murder.

"Then you have nothing to worry about," he says.

He races down the stairs, away from me. I wonder though. How innocent is Leo in all of this? His behavior seems over the top to me. Why is he so eager to throw me under the bus? And as I watch him go, I hear Marcus Snyder's voice ringing in my ears:

All you need for reasonable doubt is another plausible suspect.

WHEN I GET HOME, I remember the call from Greg Masters. I still need to connect with Sam and figure out where we go from here. I want to keep the podcast gig going. Between him and Anderson's ex-girlfriend, we'll likely have enough for a second episode.

As I pull up his voicemail, I see there's another message, from work. I'm not ready to hear what they have to say, but I'm sure it's not good news. Rather than listening to it, I call Greg Masters. He picks up, like he's been staring at the phone, waiting for me to call.

And it makes sense as to why he's doing that. Like me, he's been unfairly accused, and even though he's cleared for now, he's probably as anxious as I am to find the real killer and erase the cloud of suspicion still hovering over him.

He tells me something.

Something that could be important.

Shayna ran into Kimo Fernandez a week before she called off the wedding. She told Greg that she wasn't involved with Kimo and she didn't want to be. It's that seeing an ex who she was once in love with made her realize she wasn't in love with him.

"Did she ever say anything about him being violent with her?" I ask.

"Not that she told me. He cheated on her, though. More than once. And he had a temper, she said, especially when she called him out on it. But she never said he got physical with her."

"That doesn't mean he didn't," I point out.

"You can talk to some of her girlfriends," he suggests. Greg Masters gives me names and numbers of two women who she is close with, who might know more than he does.

It can't be a complete coincidence that Shayna saw Kimo a week before she disappeared, and that Kimo also has a connection to Tina, who also disappeared. And now he's conveniently on vacation, off the grid.

Anything to deflect attention from me is a win, so I call Sam and fill him in. We decide to meet first thing tomorrow morning before my shift and find a time to interview Greg Masters. But do I even have a shift?

So, I listen to the message and find out I've been placed on temporary leave without pay. I can keep my health insurance. At least I'm not fired. But I have hardly any savings. Sam didn't pay me anything for the first episode yet. He said he needed to gauge the response, and if it was better than normal, he'd give me a share of the ad revenue.

And now that the response was phenomenal, I'll press him for my fair share. It's probably not much, but maybe it'll tide me over. And with nowhere else to turn, I call Linda

Chun, the great listener, hoping to get some much-needed sympathy.

"Johnny," she says. "I was just thinking about you. How was your day?"

I fill her in on all of the breaking news, and she comes back with something that actually helps.

"I know how you feel, being unfairly accused. I was on the boat with my husband when he fell in. I tried to save him. Radioed for help. But still. People talked. Especially his kids, even though they got more of his estate than I did."

I knew about her being on the boat. She and her sister. "Didn't your sister vouch for you?"

"Of course," she says. "But then people accused her of being in on it with me. Which was so stupid. We didn't have a prenup. If I wanted out, I could have divorced him and gotten more than I did when he died."

"People suck," I say.

"Not all people," she says. "You don't suck, Johnny. And I'd love to see you again, before I leave."

"I'd like that, too," I say.

"I'm leaving first thing tomorrow morning."

We dance around the issue, but a pang of desire hits me as I think about her silky hair and smooth skin. The coy school girl who, over senior year, grew into her budding sexuality, and the awkward teen guy who fumbled his way through it, pretending he knew what was what, and hoping she didn't know better that he didn't.

Maybe Linda Chun *is* the one. Wouldn't that be poetic? Reconnecting with my first love? Someone who knew my family. My parents. My history, which aside from Uncle Mel has been mostly wiped out.

Throwing caution to the wind, I say, "How about now?"

"Now works for me," she says. "See you shortly."

THIRTY-THREE
JOHNNY

Linda Chun has learned a few moves since high school.

Best case scenario, we all have.

The thing is, reuniting in adulthood with somebody you knew when you were a clumsy teen creates an awkward awareness of what must have transpired in the time since you've been with them. Everyone has a past, especially at my age. But when you start out with someone at age thirty, you don't tend to be so aware of that fact. It's just them. It's how they were born, you tell yourself. You don't need to think about how they got there.

It got in the way a little, the meta observation I was having as things heated up. It was good. Great, even. And I suppose after a while the feeling would fade, if we were to continue seeing each other. But Linda left for San Diego this morning and right now, I think that's for the best. I'm in no position to start a new relationship now, especially a long distance one.

On the bright side, since I no longer have a job to go to, I am free to meet with Sam. We're putting together a second episode. *Where's Kimo?*

And I need to talk money with him. I'm not sure how long

the retainer for Marcus Snyder is good for, and I only have about a month of savings to cover my expenses. I have vacation time saved up though, about two weeks, so I put in for that, and hopefully by the time that's used up, things will be cleared up as far as my legal troubles and I can go back to work.

Either it'll be cleared up or I'll have a new place to live, courtesy of the tax payers of our state. I let out a chuckle and think that maybe I'm losing it. I didn't get high last night. I was too busy with Linda. But I'm not sure I can get through the anxiety of what's going on in my life without a little help from my friend.

Maybe I need a support group.

I hear they have those in prison.

———

SAM and I sit out by the pool at my place, going over our notes. It's a round little wading pool. Good for a dip but not the type you can do laps in. But it's pleasant and blue, and it calms me, looking at the sun reflecting off the water, with palm trees swaying in the breeze. An umbrella shades our table, keeping us comfortable this mid-morning.

The resident manager skims the pool and flashes me a wave. I wonder if he's heard the news; if everybody knows my business, or if it just feels that way because of what happened at work. If he knows, he's not saying anything. Jimmy's a pretty cool guy. I'd be disappointed if he thought I was a murderer.

Sam put together a basic script for the part where he's going to talk about Derek Anderson's freaky sex life. People love that kind of stuff so it should be a hit. I exchange text messages with Greg Masters and set up an in-person interview for late this afternoon. I've got messages out to Shayna McCarthy's girlfriends, and I'm still waiting to hear back from them.

We've pretty much got the show fleshed out, and I'm unsure how to broach the subject of payment. Instead of beating around the bush, I blurt it out.

"Hey Sam? We talked about me getting a share of the ad revenue of the show if it worked. I think it worked. I wouldn't ask you if I had a choice. But I'm not working right now, and I could use the money."

"Oh shit. Thanks for reminding me. I've got a check for you." He hands me what looks like a personal check, folded in half. "It's twenty-five percent of the revenue, which is what we agreed to. This goes for any episodes we co-host."

"Great!" I don't remember agreeing on twenty-five percent, but I'm fine with a quarter of the ad revenue. I pluck the check from his fingertips.

"We can get you set up with an online payment app, but I wanted to give you this now, since you're in a tough spot."

Then he mentions something about filling out a 1099 and hands me some paperwork. I page through it: a non-disclosure agreement and a contract of sorts. He mentions that there's no guarantee of any work with him after we finish this case. Something about ongoing expectations, and that I shouldn't have any. It sounds rehearsed, like something his lawyer told him to say.

Before I tuck it into my pocket, I open it—and try not to let my eyes pop any further out of my head. *Holy crap.* It's more than I make at the Royal in a month, not counting tips.

I think back on what my attorney said, the fact that he had Sam slated for my reasonable doubt on Derek Anderson. We'll have to find another scapegoat, because I'm not about to bite the hand that feeds me right now, even if he could be a serial killer or an axe murderer or the reincarnation of Jack the Ripper. "That's a nice payday," I say.

"I told you. I'm serious as a heart attack about my business.

Now let's get this episode done because there's more where that came from."

"Amen to that, bro," I say. "So. Where's Kimo?"

"I don't know, but where ever he is, for now, he's money in our pockets, so let's get this produced and out to my listeners before someone else finds him."

It's been years since I've been up to the North Shore. It's about the furthest you can get from where I live on this island, and with traffic and the fact that I work so much, I rarely make the time to drive up here. But now that I have no job, combined with the remote but real possibility that I might end up in prison, my wanderlust has returned.

About the time I was born, the sugar mill in Waialua went bust and the tall cane stacks that covered the landscape here were felled for the last time, somewhat replaced by local farm-to-table start-ups. For the most part, though, the region remains unchanged from what it was thirty years ago, resisting the development that has reshaped other areas of the islands.

I left earlier than I needed to. It's over an hour drive from Honolulu, on a good day. On a bad day, well, the traffic is LA-level horrible, especially in the fall and winter during surf season, or if you hit rush hour in town.

I'm at a beach park now, but not one of the touristy ones famous for the big surf, which is not currently on display. I'm on the western side at a lesser known but strikingly beautiful area of the island that seems timeless and untouched.

My main reason for being up here today is to talk to Janice, but I'm taking some time to enjoy the scenery and take a dip in the clear aqua tide pool surrounded by chunks of black reef that break the surf and keep predators away. The water up here smells fresh and crisp, different from the crowded south shore beaches, where the sea is filled with sun screen and boat run-off, and who knows what else.

I had a friend who, for about a month, thought she was dying. It turned out to be the wrong diagnosis, and she wasn't. But she told me that during that time, it gave her a new lease on life. Every sunrise. Every rainbow. Every stolen glance felt poignant. Important, like it might be her last one.

I'm not dying, but the thought of being incarcerated is having a similar effect on me. It's as if all my senses are heightened, like I'm trying to record each moment. Preserve it, in case my memories will be all I have to sustain me when I'm sitting in a prison cell.

Maybe that sounds dramatic, but who knows what will happen. I doubt they'll pin Anderson's murder on me, but innocent people get convicted all the time. And then there are the skeletons in my closet, which brings me back to Janice, and why I'm trying to run into her.

She has no idea that I'm going to be here, and I don't know for sure that she's coming today. I scored a ticket for this Sunday's polo match, hoping to catch her at the game. She's got season's tickets, and she's a devotee of the sport. Polo is big in this state, and she's not quite a fanatic, but close. I'm sure she'll show. But if she doesn't, I still plan to stay and enjoy the festivities. Locals make it into a big production. Like I said, *carpe diem*.

The game is played on an oceanfront field, with the sea

stretching out before us and the rugged Waianae mountains sitting behind, piercing the sky in the distance. Any way you stand or turn or walk, the beauty of the area commands your attention. Large lots. Some ranches, with white picket fences dotting the main road that leads out to Ka'ena point.

I used to camp out here as a kid. The area's known for night marchers: ancient warrior ghosts who roam the area at certain times of the year. If you look them in the eye, you die, and the only way to save yourself is to lie flat on your face and let them pass. I never had the misfortune of running into one, but the stories scared the crap out of me when I was little, which was the point. What's a campout without ghost stories? Only these are more than ghost stories, and trust me on this one. You don't want to mess with a night marcher.

Gates open at eleven, although the first game is at two. But people come early and tailgate. Party. Socialize. Whole families. Singles. Everything in between. There's VIP seating, but that doesn't mean much. There are no stadium seats, only a tent covering some folding chairs.

Polo is a tradition here, dating back to the late eighteen hundreds. It's kind of unclear how it started. There's a story, which could be an urban legend, about an Australian cowboy who introduced the sport when he moved here after spending time in India. But it's also been explained as result of the Paniolo tradition and the love of horses in the islands. Then there's the British influence. The Brits tried to put their stamp on the islands, before the overthrow and American annexation. Whatever it was, it stuck.

I wander around the grounds, watching the riders warm up their elegant animals.

Soon, I see Janice, and meander over her way.

"Are you stalking me?" she says, but there's a wry smile on her face.

"Maybe you rubbed off on me," I say.

"I tried for two years to get you to come with me. Now you're a polo fan?"

"I did go with you," I say.

"Twice. When we were first dating."

"So it's a delayed reaction. What can I say?" I throw up my hands.

Janice puts her hands on her hips. "Why are you here, Johnny?"

"Can't a guy just show up at a polo game for no reason?"

"Not this guy," she says.

And then she brushes my bicep with her fingernails, and a charge runs through me.

"Let's get a drink," I say. "And then I'll fill you in. Somewhere more private."

She orders a gin and tonic, and I opt for a Kona Longboard. She tells me she's meeting someone here, and my stomach sinks. I'm not over Janice, but I want to be. Then I shuttle her over to a shady spot under a tree, away from the crowd. The match will start in twenty minutes so we don't have much time.

I fill her in on my experience down at the station. Then I ask her again what really happened with those cufflinks, explaining to her that they accused me of stealing them and replacing them the night I found Derek Anderson dead.

"They might start looking through security footage surrounding the house for the weeks before his death. They're interviewing neighbors. What we did might come out. I wanted you to know that if it does, it won't be from me. I'll protect you, Janice. As much as I can."

She lets out a deep breath and stares into space for a while. "If they found the cufflinks, then all it would be is unlawful entry. We didn't take anything. If we get caught, we can tell them we broke in because you suspected him of being a serial killer. We could probably make a deal. It might not even be a felony."

"No," I say. "I thought of that. The timing is off. We broke into Anderson's house before Lani Lum went missing. It wouldn't make any sense. Keep quiet and let it blow over. I think we may be close to figuring out who killed him, and then that'll all go away."

She agrees, and for the first part of the match, we laugh and banter and cheer on our team, and it almost feels like we're back together. There are only four players on each side, but the thundering of huffs pounding on the ground and the constant back and forth movement make it feel like a stampede. The earth shakes and people cheer and yell. We keep our eyes peeled on the game, and I almost put my arm around her, because I forget for a moment that we're broken up.

But then she waves over her friend, and I'm happy that it's a woman, one I've never met. Even though I already slept with someone else, I'd hate to see Janice with another guy. No introductions are made as the friend sits in the seat Janice has saved, to her other side from where I'm seated. My former girlfriend turns her back to me.

At the first break, I excuse myself. Janice doesn't notice.

I drive in silence all the way back to Diamond Head, barely noticing the scenery that seemed so precious to me on the drive up here.

THIRTY-FIVE

JOHNNY

After smoking a quarter of a joint and flushing it down the toilet, I crack open a beer, put my feet up on the coffee table, aim the remote at the TV, and prepare to zone out.

But as I do, a call comes in from an unknown number, but one that looks vaguely familiar to me. I perk up, thinking it could be one of Shayna McCarthy's friends.

And I'm delighted to discover that it is. Her name is Kainani, and she was slated to be the maid of honor in a wedding that never happened. After a little back and forth about me and why she should even be talking to me about her friend, I convince her that, out of anyone, I have a vested interest in finding out what's going on, and that my podcast could be helpful.

Then I ask her if Shayna said anything to her about running into her old flame Kimo Fernandez the week before she called off the wedding.

"Oh yeah," she says. "She told me about that. But that's not why she called off the wedding. How did you know about that?"

"Her fiancé told me," I say. "I mean her ex-fiancé.

Although Kainani grew up here, she and Shayna only met a few years ago, at work, so she doesn't know much about her time with Kimo. She didn't know her back then. "You've been talking to Greg?" she asks.

"Yes. Why? Is there something I should know about Greg?"

"Nothing in particular. I reached out to him, trying to soften the blow of the break up before the murder, but he didn't return my call. Even at her funeral, he came with his mother for the ceremony but left without saying a word to anyone."

"As a person who has been in his shoes, I understand why he would do that. His attorney probably told him not to talk to anybody. Do you have any reason to believe he would harm your friend?"

"No, but then you never really know what's going on between two people, do you? But he certainly had no reason to harm that other woman. Don't serial killers go after strangers? That way they're harder to catch."

"I'm not an expert in that area. I'm trying to make sense of why three women with a connection to the Royal went missing, and two of them turned up dead."

"Do you think it could be this Kimo guy? I didn't hear anything about him knowing Lani Lum. And Shayna wasn't scared of him or anything."

"I have no idea. But I'm trying to find my coworker. His wife, Tina Fernandez. They were in the middle of a messy divorce. He came to the hotel where Tina and I work, looking for her, and he got in my face. So maybe he had nothing to do with the other two murders, but maybe he had something to do with Tina's disappearance. Maybe her case isn't related to the murders and maybe it is. Did Shayna ever say anything about him being violent?"

"No. He was a cheater, she said. A real lady killer. It

messed up her head. She had a hard time trusting guys for a while, but then she met Greg. Greg was gaga about her, but I never got the feeling she felt that way about him. But that's probably why she agreed to marry him. He was safe. And I'm not surprised that she broke it off. Safe isn't very sexy, or very sustainable."

"Greg said that Kimo had a temper. Do you know anything about that?"

"I would be very surprised if Shayna had talked to Greg about Kimo. And no, she never said he was violent. Just a jerk who was way too full of himself, and she didn't understand how she could still feel physically attracted to him, that day when she ran into him at the supermarket and they talked. I told her that chemistry doesn't have to make sense. But she did tell me she was interested in someone else. A guy she knew from her college days on the continent, who she ran into by chance. He asked her for coffee, and she wanted to meet up with him, which told her that she couldn't marry Greg."

"A guy she used to date?"

"No," Kainani says. "I don't think so. Why? Do you think he could have something to do with what happened to her?"

"It's anyone's guess. Like you said, most serial killers don't go after women they know well, but sometimes they go after women they date."

There's a long pause, and then she says, "I listened to your podcast."

"What did you think?"

"It was entertaining, I guess. But if you ever want to do a more victim-centered episode about what Shayna was like, you can call me. She was my best friend, and as much as I want her killer to be caught, I also want her to be remembered for something other than the way she... d...d...died." There's silence as

Kainani swallows a sob. After a bit, she adds, "I'm sorry. I still can't believe this is happening."

This hits me hard. The sadness in her voice. The way she choked up at the end. It makes me realize that Shayna McCarthy isn't simply a headline. She's someone's friend. Someone's daughter. Not just someone's victim.

"Maybe I can do something on both of the women."

"I'd like that," she says.

But of course, my mind is reeling with this new information. A guy she met in college, who she ran into recently. Could it be?

"Hey Kainani. One more thing. Where did Shayna go to college?"

"Pomona," she says. "In So Cal. Why?"

"You said she ran into someone she knew in college, so it might be helpful to have that information, in case something hits me."

"I doubt the guy she ran into has anything to do with her murder. To my knowledge, she never actually went out on a date with him."

But that's what she told her friend. Maybe she went out with him on the down-low. If she did meet up with him, that could piss off a guy like Greg Masters, who seems almost inhumanly forgiving. But what would Masters have against Lani Lum?

As we're getting off the phone, she says, "But if you're going down that road, you should also know she went to Stanford for grad school."

My eyes pop open.

Derek Anderson went to Stanford.

But if I am right, if he was the one behind this after all, then two burning questions remain unanswered:

Who killed him?
And where is Tina Fernandez?

THIRTY-SIX
JOHNNY

Sam isn't too interested in a victim-centered podcast on the two murdered women, and this nags at me. It seems a little callous, like he's in it just for the payday. Like, he doesn't actually realize that people were murdered. Real people, with families and lives ahead of them. I wonder if he was always like that, or if the money has gone to his head. Maybe that's what happens over time.

I make a silent vow that I won't forget the victims if I keep doing this kind of work. That's why I held back a little on disclosing parts of my conversation with Kainani to Sam. I told him that she verified what Greg Masters told me about Shayna running into Kimo, but he doesn't have room for another interview with her for this upcoming episode. Sam says he'll add in the fact that Greg's claim was verified by an additional source. He plans to upload the episode tonight, and that's fine with me.

I've got a busy day ahead of me. First, I'm going to check in with Uncle Mel. Then I'm going on a little getaway, even though I was warned not to leave town. I've got a hunch about something, and I need to check it out on my own.

MEL and I meet at the Honu Club again, but this time, he ushers me straight to a table. We sit with our coffees, which we get from a self-serve area. They're not serving food yet, and the dining room is nearly empty except for a few singles, texting on their phones and an older couple sitting in comfortable silence gazing out at the surfers and the paddlers in the distance.

It's clear that we're here to discuss business. No back-slapping introductions to the fellas, who aren't even here yet. The bar is closed. He picked the time. Mel's not happy with me about the podcast. He's not eager to show me off to his cronies today.

"You know what it means to be your own worst enemy?" he says.

"I get what you're saying, but—"

He holds up a hand. "No buts. Just listen to me for once. Your generation. Can't tell you anything. I told you to lie low. You think that's laying low? Broadcasting yourself to millions of listeners?"

"Not millions. One point eight million." I smirk.

Mel remains stone-faced, clearly not in the mood for humor. "And, you got yourself fired."

"I'm not fired," I offer. "I'm on temporary leave."

"Same difference," he says. "Even Marcus Snyder's annoyed with you."

"I didn't kill Derek Anderson," I reassert. "That's why I said I'd take a polygraph. I thought it would make me look innocent."

"You never know what could happen in those situations. It was foolish. Hopefully you learned something from it."

"I did," I say, telling Mel what he wants to hear, because in my mind, the strategy worked just fine.

"Any news on how Derek Anderson was murdered?" I ask.

"He was shot. You already know this."

"Yeah. But with what?"

"They aren't sharing that with me. Why? You got an illegal weapon somewhere?"

"No! Of course not. I'm just wondering. My attorney didn't mention it. Shouldn't he be able to find that out?"

"Not if you haven't been arrested."

Instead of harping on the Derek Anderson case, I change the subject to Kimo Fernandez and warn Mel about the upcoming episode and the bombshell revelation that he also has a connection to Shayna McCarthy. I remind him that Kimo could have done something to Tina, and tell Mel that I'm concerned about Tina's disappearance, hoping to impress upon him that this isn't all about me.

Uncle Mel is not impressed.

"Son," he says. "I don't know how many ways I can tell you the same thing. If you want to solve crimes, HPD is hiring. But this isn't the way to do it, playing amateur detective and wasting your time with this ridiculous podcast gig instead of looking for a new job."

"Podcasting is a job. Sam pays me," I say. But I don't want to let him know how lucrative it is for fear of seeming like a parasite to Mel, so I add, "It's not much, but it'll tide me over. And those shows help catch killers. They keep eyes on the cases, especially the cold ones."

"This isn't a cold case. It's an active investigation. And you're a person of interest in one of the murders."

"Noted. But an opportunity presented itself, and I'm taking it. I'm not going to be a valet driver for the rest of my life."

"So, you're going to be a true crime podcaster for the rest of your life? That's your plan?"

I shrug. "Maybe. I want to do a show about the victims, but Sam doesn't want to, so I'm thinking I'll do it myself."

"That's a noble sentiment. But do you know anything about the business?"

Shrugging, I say, "I've got time on my hands. I can learn."

And as we wrap up and he asks me to promise him that I won't meddle any further in the investigation, all I can say is, "I'll be careful, Uncle Mel. And I do respect you. More than you know."

THIRTY-SEVEN
JOHNNY

I was half-expecting the TSA agent to call for back-up when I showed him my license to get through security, but I guess I'm not that notorious. The flight time is only twenty minutes or so, but it still takes half a day or more to get from point A to point B, by the time you drive to the airport, park, fly over, and get your rental car.

But I'm finally in my blue Ford Focus, headed for the North Shore of Kaua'i. There was something about Auntie Marjorie's performance that bothered me, and I think she knows more than she's letting on.

She tells fortunes at a gift shop in Hanalei, a colorful little beach town a few miles past the lux Princeville resort complex, and home of world-famous Hanalei Bay. The weather turns rainy and cool as I transition to the northern part of the island, which is not uncommon. It's one of the wettest parts of the island chain, but also the most lush and green.

Mountainous and spectacular, at the far end, the pali, or cliffs, tower four thousand feet above a wild and furious sea, slicing into the churning water like a series of Santoku knives.

Its magnificence can only be truly appreciated from the air or the ocean. I've done both, and although I'm not here to vacation, good memories pop into my head.

Like the time we did a helicopter tour, and my father looked like he was going to toss his cookies. Mom laughed at him. She thrived on danger. At eight years old, I was somewhere between the two of them. In awe of what I was seeing, but keenly aware of the fact that being suspended in mid-air between a series of jagged peaks was unnatural for a human being.

I've got some time to kill, so I stop at the Westin resort in Princeville for a coffee. Janice and I came here about a year ago, on some kind of timeshare deal they had going. We stayed in a one-bedroom villa with an ocean view and an in-room jacuzzi.

How was it? It was freaking awesome, that's what it was.

We stayed on the ground floor of a three-story building. That's another nice thing about this island. Nothing can be taller than a coconut tree. And we had this pair of Nene geese who stopped by our lanai every day to visit. The species was almost wiped out in the fifties, and now they're protected and they seem to be everywhere. One of them had a little bracelet on its ankle. Not sure if it was the male or the female. The geese mate for life, Janice said, and that made me smile. Maybe it was time for me to mate for life, too, I thought, but I didn't say anything to her yet. As I said, she's the kind of woman who's hard to read.

It was a great trip, until we went to the timeshare presentation that we were required to do to get our discounted package. We didn't buy the timeshare, but we did sit through a ninety-minute presentation, which wasn't what you would think. Low key. No pressure. The setting sells itself, I guess.

But it got awkward in terms of the relationship. I thought we were serious, but when the salesperson asked if "we" wanted to move forward with a purchase, Janice let out a chuckle. "Oh," she said. "This would just be for me. We're not a 'we.' And I don't think it's a good fit for me right now."

Up until that point, we were having a great time. I was serious about her. Thinking about marriage. But that put me off a lot, and I still don't know why she was so reluctant to throw in with me. Was it my restlessness? Or was she trying not to be presumptuous? Maybe if we'd talked more back then, things would have turned out differently. Who knows. All I know is she's on my mind a lot, and I'd like to get her off of it.

I grab a coffee from the little shop we went to each morning and sit at one of the tables. The resort sits high on a cliff, and although there's no beach, it offers a great view of the deep blue ocean. That week, we drove to Hanalei Bay to swim and stroll and shop.

The setting here is relaxing and romantic, except for the chickens. We've gotten a better handle on the feral problem in Honolulu, but Kaua'i is a different story. They keep spray bottles on the table now to squirt at them, and I do. I hate those motherfuckers, especially the roosters. So loud and aggressive.

And after I've had enough of squirting chickens and reminiscing and wallowing and the thinking about what might have been, I remind myself that I'm here to solve a murder, grab my coffee, and go on my way.

AFTER FIFTEEN MINUTES or so of stop-and-go traffic and a backup at the one-lane bridge that I need to cross to get to Hanalei, I arrive at my destination, Ching Young Village. It's a strip mall of sorts that has a Big Save supermarket, boutiques, shops, and restaurants, a pizza joint, and a tattoo parlor. Massage therapists, a yoga studio, and of course, a fortune teller. No chain stores, only mom-and-pop establishments, as if time-warped from another era.

The shop where Marjorie works is an eclectic mix of upscale granola with a dash of new age: natural fiber clothing, hand-made jewelry and lotions, crystals and books on self-actualization. Hanalei was a popular hippie spot in the sixties, and it's retained that vibe. Wind chimes give it an ethereal quality as I stroll around, waiting for my appointment.

"Can I help you?" the sales lady asks. She's late middle-aged, wearing a hibiscus-flowered dress. Her soft gray hair curls loosely around her face.

"No," I say. And I explain why I'm here.

"Oh, Marjorie has such a gift. You'll love her."

Another shopper wanders in, sparing me the small talk.

Marjorie's setup is not at all what I pictured. She's got a folding table and chairs in a corner of the shop near the small dressing room, and she's doing the woman's reading right there, out in the open. I expected a room with beaded curtains, dim lighting, the smoke of burning incense curling towards my nostrils—I'm already underwhelmed.

Soon, it's my turn, and she apologizes for the tight quarters.

Marjorie looks younger than I pictured her. Around early fifties, with auburn hair she wears in a messy bun, with tendrils that hang down and cup her chin. Her nails are perfectly manicured, medium length and dark red. My gaze is drawn to them as she manipulates the deck and periodically taps on the cards with the nail of her index finger.

"We usually sit outside, but it's drizzling today," she explains, as if that would be an improvement. She charges a hundred bucks, and you have to sit outside? Must be a lot of desperate people out there. Still, I smile as she shuffles her tarot card deck. Sam didn't say anything about Marjorie using tarot cards.

"We're doing a three-card spread today, using the major arcana," she says, as if that means something to me. "That's always best to start, and if you want to continue, I can follow up virtually and we can get into your life in more detail, in a more private setting."

I guess that's how she scores clients. Reel them in with some general information, and then get them hooked with the fine print.

She closes her eyes, breathing in and out, her fingertips brushing over the deck of cards, which she is no longer shuffling.

"What do you want to know?" she says. "Why are you here?"

I shrug. "Isn't that what you tell me?"

"That's not how this works. The cards are here to guide you. Give you insight. Are you at some kind of crossroads?"

"Sure," I say, trying not to smirk.

Some soothsayer. Everyone's at some kind of crossroad.

"Regarding?" she asks.

"Huh?"

"Romance? Family? Work?"

Just throw some spaghetti on the wall and see what sticks. I guess that's how she rolls. "Let's try work," I say.

She cuts the deck a few times, then puts three cards face down. "Ready?" she asks.

I nod.

Turning them over one by one, I read them:

Justice. The fool. The magician.

Justice and the magician look exactly as you might expect. But the fool is harder to read, and I'm thinking it's not a great one to get: a young guy looking aimless, on some kind of journey, with a little dog in his hand. Janice would have a field day with this.

Marjorie looks to me and says, "Don't worry. These are all perfectly fine cards. But before I read each one, I need to give you the general gist of what I see here. All of these have to do with decision-making. Justice represents your past. It could indicate that you've made some bad decisions, ones that require repentance. It doesn't always mean that, but taken in context of the other cards, that would be my best guess. The fool represents your present, the folly of youth and the reluctance to make a commitment. But ending on the magician as your future shows me that you're on the verge of some very positive changes. Decisions that could move you forward, to a place of maturity. But something is holding you back."

"Right," I say. "Any idea what that could be?" This time, I can't stop a smirk from creeping up my face.

"I can sense that you're skeptical about this process, but there must be some reason you're dishing out a hundred bucks to talk to me today. What exactly is it you want to know, Ryan? The more precise the question, the more I can try to interpret these cards for you."

I didn't use my real name, but for some reason, I feel like she might be on to me. My face hasn't been in the public eye, but Sam did put my photo in the bio for our episode. I had a baseball cap on my head, and I look different bald. But still. I'm sure she listened to the podcast.

"I'm thinking of a career change, but it's a little risky. And my ex-girlfriend told me that I'm a grass is greener kind of person. That I always want what I don't have. I'm wondering if that's true. What do the cards say?"

"The cards tell me that you're on the brink of something positive. Whatever you're thinking about, it's a good path forward. But the justice card can indicate a legal problem, too. Sometimes the cards are more literal. Do you have a legal issue?"

"Me? Nah." I shake my head. "Nothing like that."

Marjorie spends the next twenty minutes or so trying to upsell me on more sessions, but I still can't shake the feeling that she's fishing for information. That she might suspect that I'm here for a totally different reason. That she might have listened to the podcast and she's trying to determine if I'm the same guy.

And now I know for sure what my next move should be. I need to go to her house and see if Tina's hiding out there. If perhaps Marjorie is more invested in her niece's safety than she let on with Sam.

THIRTY-EIGHT
JOHNNY

After my tarot card reading, I stop to grab some food at a little plate lunch place. The girl at the counter looks about sixteen, but she could be older. She's a bigger girl with adorable, deep dimples and an infectious smile, and I get this pang out of nowhere.

A dad pang.

A pang that tells me I want to have a daughter like her someday. A daughter who is polite and hard-working, or even one who's a pain in the ass. A daughter I can protect and love and cherish, whether she's fat or thin or has horrible acne, which this girl doesn't, but you get my drift.

A young guy who runs the food from the kitchen to the register places an eco-friendly container on the counter for the middle-aged woman in front of me.

"Do you need a bag, auntie?" the girl says.

"No, no. No need," the lady says.

She's not the girl's auntie. It's just a term of respect kids use for older people, like ma'am.

Soon it's my turn. I order the chicken katsu plate, with

white rice, mac salad and a few carrot slices to make you feel not so bad about the carbs. Comfort food is what I need right now, and this hits the spot. I wait while it's dished out into the container, and soon the guy slaps it down.

"Would you like a bag, uncle?" she says.

Wow. Am I old enough to be called uncle?

I guess to a teenager I am.

Now that is a wake-up call.

"No need," I say.

On my drive back towards Marjorie's house and the airport, I send a voice text to Sam, letting him know that I'm doing some more research on the case. I tell him I did a tarot session with Auntie Marjorie on Kaua'i. I recorded it, I add. Easy to do in a one-party state. I'm learning. He's always hounding me about that.

No audio, no podcast.

It's become his mantra.

But I don't tell him where I'm headed next, or anything about my theory about where Tina might be and what I think happened. If I'm right, I want all the credit. I don't want to live in his shadow forever. If I break this case, I'll be famous. And if he doesn't want to do victim-centered podcasts, that's fine with me, because I do. And Tina is the only victim I personally know, so I plan to start there.

I'm getting close.

I can feel it.

ABOUT TWENTY MINUTES into my thirty-minute drive, I get a call from Uncle Mel. I let it go to voicemail. A few minutes later, I pull into a shopping plaza and listen to what he has to say. Mel tells me that he heard from one of his cop buddies that Janice came in to talk to the detectives about Derek Anderson and implores me to call him.

He doesn't mention if this was her idea or if they told her to come in, but this gets my pulse racing. Either way, it's not good. This means either they found some footage or a witness or something to reveal that we broke into his house, or Janice is doing something to double-cross me. Maybe she's more pissed off about Linda Chun than she let on.

But I'm not letting this news stop me. I hope to solve the murder of Derek Anderson today and clear myself. Rather than call Mel back, I continue to Kapa'a, following the map and the address I got off the internet for Marjorie's house, hoping that the listing is current.

I turn off Kuhio Highway and onto a bypass road that meanders back towards the foothills. The area is surprisingly rural, given that it's just off the main road. Overgrown grass and bamboo shoots sit in front of mature trees of various heights, providing lots of cover. It's a great place to hide out, although it's pretty close to the police station, for someone not wanting that kind of attention.

I arrive at the address I plugged into my app. A tan Honda Civic sits on the lawn in front of the house; there's no driveway. It looks too old to be a rental car, which makes sense. If Tina murdered Derek Anderson in self-defense and is hiding here, she would not want to be too obvious.

As I'm parking my rental car in front of Marjorie's weathered plantation-style home, I get another text from Mel. He tells me to call him. It's something important, he says, but I can't very well call him now.

Sneaking around the side of the house, I first try looking in the window. Of course, I could be wrong about Tina, but I have a back-up plan. If Marjorie is here and she really doesn't know where Tina is, I'll come out and tell her that I work with Sam and I wanted to see if Tina was here, perhaps hiding from her violent husband.

"Tina?" I call out as a knock on the front door. "It's me. Johnny. I want to help," I say. "I know about Derek Anderson and what a creep he was. Whatever happened between the two of you, it's understandable. You don't have to run. Let me help you."

No response.

My feet crunch along the gravel pathway that leads around the rear of the house. There's a back door that has two steps up and a landing, so I hop up and look in the window at the top of the door, into the kitchen. The light is on but nobody is there. A pot sits on the stove, and I can't tell if it's turned on.

I pull out my phone to dial Tina's number and see if I can hear it ring or buzz, and I see a text from Sam, responding to my earlier one:

> Kimo was found dead with a suicide note
> confessing to the murders. Probably staged.
> Be careful.

Before I can process this bombshell information, I sense someone sneaking up behind me. Whipping my head around, I see a baseball bat barreling towards my head. I duck, then I catch my balance and try to grab the bat from her.

She pulls it away just in time and swings at me from the other direction.

The wood cracks into my skull with a deafening thud. The pain is immediate and unbearable. It's everywhere, reverberating from my head, down my spine, to the tips of my toes, sapping my energy and making my head spin.

In a last-ditch effort to save myself, I hurl myself towards her.

We both fall and tumble off the stoop, and our heads

collide. Then my head hits the ground, and searing pain shoots through me once again.

The last thing I see before I pass out is Marjorie staring down at me with a terrified look on her face, blood dripping from her forehead.

———

WHEN I COME TO, I'm tied to a chair, a rag stuffed loosely into my mouth. My vision blurs as I try to focus on my surroundings. I hear Marjorie talking in a forceful whisper. I shut my eyes and lean my head to the side so she doesn't know I'm awake.

Wiggling my hands, I try to loosen the rope and free myself. I think I can do it, if I'm careful and I have enough time. She probably didn't have the strength to tighten it too much, but I can't let her on to the fact that I'm awake and trying to free myself. Blood trickles down my face and into my mouth. I wonder if my injuries could be fatal.

"I didn't sign on for this, Tina!" Marjorie says. "I didn't sign on for murder. It's your mess, and you need to come clean it up. I want my payday, and then I want you out of my life."

My brain is in a fog, but I try to push through it. Something important happened right before she attacked me, but I can't remember what it was. It hurts my head to try to remember, so I focus on what I know.

I was right that Marjorie is helping Tina. But helping her do what? It's also clear that Marjorie isn't capable of murder, or she would have finished me off. She's leaving that to Tina, and I have no idea where Tina is, or when she'll come clean up her mess.

I've got two choices. I can fake sleep and try to free myself. Try to overpower Marjorie and call for help, hoping that Tina is far enough away that I have enough time, and that Tina didn't bring her gun to Kaua'i. Or I can try to appeal to Marjorie's sense of decency and get her to turn on her niece.

Before I can weigh my options, a violent eruption seizes me, and soon my plate lunch comes out the way it went in, popping the rag out with it.

Marjorie whips her head towards me, her eyes wild with panic.

"I need medical attention, Marjorie."

"You shut the hell up!" she thunders. "This was self-defense. You were breaking into my house." But her heart's not in it, and it's possible she's more terrified than I am. This is not a woman who wants a murder on her rap sheet.

She paces the floor, sweating, wringing her hands like an aging witch, her reddish hair disheveled, matching the dried blood on her face, which I realize is probably mine. It's clear that Marjorie is motivated by money, so a wild idea pops into my throbbing head.

"Marjorie. I've got an idea," I say. "An idea that could make us both a lot of money, and get you off the hook in the process."

She stops pacing and crosses her arms, eyeing me.

"Go on," she says.

And I do.

THIRTY-NINE
JOHNNY

Tina glares at me, syringe in hand, as I sit in a chair, hands behind my back.

"Why did you have to go meddle in my business? I like you, Johnny. I didn't want this to happen. I told you. I can take care of myself."

Her face sports a nasty bruise, as does her forearm, which looks like a vise was clamped around it. Her wrists look like she was bound to a chair, like me.

No gun, which I already knew from Marjorie. Because Tina used her nine-millimeter to kill Derek Anderson and then dumped it in Paiko Lagoon, like she did with Lani Lum's body. She used her husband's gun to stage his suicide, after jabbing him with a syringe of insulin to make him more manageable. His mother's insulin, which also killed the two women.

She's still got a stash of the drug, which she plans to use on me.

"You'll never get away with it," I tell Tina as she readies the syringe. "Once they know I died of an insulin overdose like the women, they'll figure it out. We could go to the cops. Tell them it was self-defense, like that burning bed woman. Kimo trauma-tized you. The cheating. The abuse. Derek Anderson was a freak. You snapped. They'll take that into consideration."

"Shut up, Johnny," she says. "Maybe I don't like you so much after all. And don't worry, they'll never find your body. Marjorie's got a lot of land in back of the house."

"Oh, no you don't," Marjorie says. "You're not dumping a body here."

"Just until we get the money, stupid. They'll find Kimo's body and the note soon. It won't be long. Then we're in the clear. It's millions, Marjorie. I'll get his life insurance, too. Think about it. We could leave the country. Start over."

"Did Derek Anderson try to hurt you?" I ask, trying to connect with her humanity.

"Derek Anderson was a filthy pig!" Tina thunders. "He asked me to do unspeakable things. And when I wouldn't, he called me pathetic. Said I should take what I could get from a guy like him. That he was way out of my league, and I should be *grateful* that he asked. Grateful!"

"So you executed him?" I say, still mildly pleased with myself that I was right about the scumbag all along.

"It was fast. And painless, just like the others. I'm not inhu-mane, Johnny. I'm not a sadist or anything. So don't worry. It'll be like that with you, too. I'm sorry it's come to this."

As Tina lunges at me with the syringe, I spring up, knock the death needle out of her hand, and wrap my arms around her.

"Okay, Marjorie. We've got the recording. Call the cops," I say.

Tina hisses to her aunt: "I'll kill you, too, Marjorie. I'll find a way. You know I will. Don't you dare touch that phone."

Marjorie's eyes dart around the room as Tina wriggles in my arms. And instead of her phone, Marjorie grabs the syringe and rushes towards me. I guess I should have seen this coming. I saw Marjorie's eyes light up when Tina mentioned millions of dollars. I can't offer her nearly that much, and she's terrified of her niece.

Now it's two against one. I shove Tina down to the floor as Marjorie comes at me with the needle. I know she's weak and vulnerable, so I knock it out of her hand and stomp on the syringe. Then I shove her down hard, and she crashes to the floor.

Spinning around to face my other attacker, I duck as Tina swings at me with the baseball bat, still crusted with my blood. The movement makes me dizzy, and nausea nearly paralyzes me. One more blow to the head and I'm as good as dead.

The ground beneath me shifts, and I know I'm on the verge of passing out. I think about the fact that my recorder is still on when I hear sirens in the background. If I can hold the line for a few minutes, this could still work out.

Tina stops in her tracks and turns to Marjorie. "Did you call the cops, you stupid cow?"

The look on Marjorie's face tells me she's more afraid of her niece than she is of prison. "I didn't. I swear!"

She didn't. She couldn't have. And I have no idea who did.

Maybe a neighbor?

Tina explodes. "Everyone betrays me! Even you. We're family!" She lunges towards Marjorie with the bat, swinging at her like a lunatic. I try to grab it, even though one more blow to my head will probably kill me. But she's going to kill Marjorie if I don't stop her.

The bat grazes the side of Marjorie's head, and Marjorie goes down. I know I could grab my recorder and run, but I can't do it. I can't let Tina beat Marjorie to death. I'd never be able to live with the guilt.

Ducking Tina's swings as I fight down the bile, I finally

grab the bat, spin Tina around, shove her down, and pin her to the ground with the bat and my foot. Hopefully, Marjorie's not stupid enough to double-cross me again.

But Marjorie can barely get up, I see. She's not a threat to me.

The sirens are closer now, clearly headed our way.

Tina writhes and gyrates under my feet, and my strength is waning. I don't know how long I can hold her down. I could hit her again, but it's not that easy to do with her staring up at me. She's a woman, smaller and weaker than me.

So I try something else. "Why did you do it, Tina?" I ask. "Was it only about the money?"

The sirens wail as the cop cars peel into the yard, bathing us in red and blue strobe lighting that makes everything feel surreal.

Car doors slam.

It's over, and Tina knows it.

Her face softens, and the crazed look on her face vanishes before my eyes. "I loved Kimo," she says. "With all my heart. But he betrayed me. Just like Marjorie. Just like Derek Anderson. But not you, Johnny. You tried to help. You always saw the good in me. And I'm glad I didn't have to kill you, too."

The strangest thing happens as her child-like voice connects with a memory. A memory I couldn't recall from that day I was on break, near the conference room, that day they told me I was seen sitting near Shayna McCarthy.

It was Tina's voice I heard.

"Don't I know you from somewhere?" she said.

I turned to see Tina talking to someone, but Tina was blocking my view of the other person. It must have been Shayna McCarthy. Did running into Kimo's ex ignite her fury and set her on this deadly path? Give her the idea to set him up as a serial killer, stage a suicide, and take all their money?

I have to hand it to Sam.
It was a woman, after all.
I guess I had a blind spot.
Money and jealousy, the classic motives.
And now, I've got it all on tape.

FORTY

JOHNNY

Turns out, Sam probably saved my life.

I was worried the cops might shoot me, thinking I'd broken into the house, so as soon as they burst through the door, I jumped back from Tina, threw my hands up and said, "It's not how it looks. Don't shoot."

There were two of them. A guy about my age, and one maybe in his late forties. They didn't seem too interested in me.

Marjorie chimed in, trying to save herself. "He's right! My niece is a murderer. I had nothing to do with any of it. She just showed up here, and—"

Tina sprang up from the floor and hurled herself towards her auntie, but the older officer grabbed Tina and cuffed her before she could get too close.

He said, "Tina Fernandez, you're under arrest for the murder of Derek Anderson."

And I wondered why they didn't mention the other murders. I'm still wondering that, in fact. But then I got dizzy again. I staggered to the sofa and nearly passed out.

"Holy shit," the younger cop said, when he looked over at me.

Then he called for an ambulance, and that's the last thing I remember before passing out.

Now I'm at Wilcox Hospital, patched up, with an IV drip hydrating me. I've got a concussion and some swelling on the brain, but they said I should be fine if I rest up and don't push myself too hard.

Once our *Where's Kimo* episode hit the air, it seems Kimo's sister tracked Sam down, frantic and furious that the episode was so unfair to her brother.

Yes, she admitted. He was a bit of a womanizer. But Tina was the violent one.

Sam told her about the bruise I saw on her arm a while back and she said, "Yeah, well she probably got it when he was trying to grab the baseball bat out of her hand while she was swinging it at Kimo's head."

Now that, I can believe.

Of course, a sister would paint a brother that way, so at first Sam brushed it off. But when he put it together with the fact that even the cops thought Kimo's suicide looked staged, a clearer and more deranged picture of Tina emerged.

But getting back to me, and Sam saving my life. Like me, Sam thought Auntie Marjorie had given off a strange vibe. Not psychic strange, but shady strange. And when Kimo's sister mentioned that her brother wanted to divorce Tina and take half of their net worth, which would have included Tina's inheritance, something clicked for him.

Sam didn't know I was at Marjorie's house, but he tipped off the cops to the fact that he thought Tina might be hiding at her aunt's place. Marjorie seemed like an opportunist, and as Sam thought, she jumped at the chance to get a piece of the wealth.

Tina had a whole story lined up, according to her aunt. She planned to tell the cops that she fled and went into hiding because she was on to Kimo being a serial killer and he was going to kill her, too. She had evidence she'd cobbled together about the crime, which was easy to get—because she was actually the murderer.

She planned to claim that Kimo found out about her evidence and kidnapped her, and she fought him off and went into hiding. She actually pummeled herself with a tire iron in the face to get that bruise and make that part of the story believable, and she gave herself deep rope burns around her wrists to look like she'd been tied up. The handprint on the forearm, I think, came from her husband, a last-ditch effort to save himself.

In the suicide note, Kimo talked about guilt and remorse and the fact that he didn't want to go to prison, and asked for his wife's forgiveness. That part of the plan was laughable, but I have to admit, it was bold. Tina planned to resurface when Kimo turned up dead, to get her payday. The timing was nothing but dumb luck in terms of finding me at the house.

I need to heal up fast, though, and get this podcast out before it becomes old news. I've got a serial killer on a recording, confessing to murder. It doesn't get any better than that.

For now, I need to rest, so I shut my eyes for a minute, I tell myself.

But my body has others plan for me.

IT'S three hours later when I wake up. I still don't know what's going on with Marjorie and Tina, but the cop who was outside my room earlier is no longer there.

Someone walks into the room.

Someone I'm quite delighted and surprised to see.

"So, this is you, listening to my advice?" Uncle Mel says. "Young people these days. Can't tell them anything."

"You came," I say.

Mel shrugs. "It's a twenty-minute flight. It's not exactly a trip to Antarctica. Don't be so flattered."

He pulls up a chair next to my bed and sits down.

"Is this when I get the lecture?" I ask.

Mel shakes his head. "No lecture this time. In my experience, there's nothing like seeing your life flash before your eyes to get a lesson like that through someone's thick head."

"Amen to that," I say. "It was foolish."

"One man's foolish is another man's brave."

"You think I'm brave?"

Mel smirks. "I didn't say that, exactly."

But he didn't have to. I can see it on his face. He's beaming, and that makes the pounding in my head worth it.

"Hey, Mel. When they arrested Tina, they only mentioned Derek Anderson's murder. Do you know what's up with that?"

"That's probably all the DA would go for, with the evidence they had. They found the murder weapon and traced it to her. If they don't have a slam dunk indictment these days, they turn chickenshit. But with your recording, I'm sure they'll get a confession out of her for all of it, or at least enough for an indictment. Hard to believe. How did you figure it out?"

I could lie. Tell him I had the whole thing put together in my head, like Sam. But I have a new lease on life. And I want to be a better man.

"I didn't," I confess. "I thought Tina was a battered woman. And with the way she was flirting with Derek Anderson, I figured he could have been the serial killer after all, and he just messed with the wrong woman. Or he wasn't the serial killer, but he got freaky on her and she snapped, after all the domestic abuse. I had no idea she was behind it all. I didn't find out about Kimo and his staged suicide until right before Marjorie jumped me. I came here to protect Tina. To get her to turn herself in, hoping that I could get her to see with the right lawyer, this wouldn't need to be so bad."

Mel nods along, but he doesn't say anything.

"Some detective, huh? You must think I'm a sucker."

"Nobody could've seen this coming. It's one of the most bizarre cases I've seen in my entire career. You're not a sucker, Johnny. You're a good guy. And I'm proud of you."

I wonder how proud he'll be when I tell him about my taped confession, and what I'm planning to do with it. But it's my brass ring, and I'm grabbing it.

My mind flashes to the magician, my future path. Marjorie told me she started to get an inkling I was the guy from the podcast about midway through our session. That would have been after she cut the deck and dealt the cards. The magician is a good sign, she said. A sign that I'm headed to a better future.

Did she engineer that?

Is that what she says to everyone?

Do we all see what we want to see in the cards?

Or do we manifest our own futures, like the motivational experts tell us?

Whatever way I look at it, I take it as a sign. My future is mine to mold, and in the wake of my near-death experience, I'm determined to create a better one, and not only for me.

It's been two weeks since I broke the case, and my podcast episode was a huge success. I ended up cutting Sam in on the episode, not only because the guy saved my life, but also because he had all the sponsor contacts and equipment and technical expertise to make this happen fast. But this time, he's getting a quarter of the ad revenue, and I'm getting the rest.

I owned up about my suspicions about him possibly being a serial killer, and Sam just laughed. "Don't worry. I thought it was you, too, in the beginning. That's why I asked you to do the podcast with me. Keep you close."

Then he told me something he didn't need to disclose, but he did it anyway. He said the reason he left college was that he thought his roommate was behind the sexual assaults. The guy kept guns in the room. He was the incel type, and Sam thought he seemed ready to blow. Sam turned the guy in, and then Sam's parents extracted their son from what they thought was a dangerous situation. Bought his way into a better, safer place.

The women didn't want to press charges and there was no evidence pointing to the roommate as the perp, but the kid dropped out of college and vanished into thin air. That's when Sam got interested in crime and started listening to true crime podcasts. Then he got the idea to start his own business. He majored in business, focusing on entrepreneurialism and marketing so he could start his own company, which is easier to do if you have a family with deep pockets. Still, I give him credit for turning the guy in—ballsy thing to do.

We've decided to go our own ways, although he did say he'd make himself available, for a fee, to show me the ropes, and we left the door open to future collaborations. I want to make good on my promise to do victim-centered podcasts, and I'm starting with Shayna McCarthy and Lani Lum.

Turns out, Lani Lum had a connection to Kimo Fernandez, too. They all went to the same high school: Tina, Kimo, and Lani Lum. And it was only after Lani Lum turned Kimo down that he asked Tina to the prom. Tina thought it would turn into more, but it didn't. And then they graduated, and that summer, Kimo dated Shayna McCarthy instead of Tina.

Shayna didn't hang out with Lani Lum or Kimo in high school. She went to a top-tier college and was, socially, a little out of Kimo's league. But Kimo had a way with the ladies, and for a while, he had her hooked. But he strayed, and she dumped him, and Tina got her hooks in him at just the right time.

I still don't know what exactly made Tina snap, because even with the connections, I still don't see a motive for murder. Was it the repeated infidelity? A teenage obsession? Did she have it in her all along? And although I'm committed to doing victim-centered podcasts, I'm about to do an interview with Tina. I need answers. I need to know why she did what she did. She's being held without bail, and I've set up a visit. Marjorie is trying to make a deal to testify against her. That's about all I know.

Afterwards, I'm going to do some in-depth work on the

victims in this case. Then I'll work with HPD on some of their cold cases. Ones that haven't gotten as much attention as the Honolulu Strangler or the Dana Ireland cases. Ones that everyone else has forgotten about. Mel hooked me up with the new Honolulu cold case team, and I'm excited to get started as soon as I wrap up this one.

We meet in a communal visitor center at the women's correctional center, and Tina enters, wearing an orange jumpsuit that's too big for her. She looks defeated, and I can't help but feel some sympathy for her, despite the fact that she's a murderer. Would I feel this way if she were a guy? Of course not, and I need to realize that this soft spot I have for the ladies isn't doing me any favors.

She's in handcuffs, and she places her forearms on the table. I think about the fact that it could have been me, and I'm grateful that I never ended up on her side of the table.

"Hi Johnny," she says.

The voice still throws me. It's so dainty and harmless. It is not the voice of a serial killer, except that it is.

"Hi Tina," I say. "How are you holding up?"

She shrugs. "It is what it is."

There's an awkward silence as we struggle with how to begin.

"So I wanted—"

"You're here to get stuff for your podcast, right? I bet you made a lot of money off that episode," she says. "Want to get the crazy lady on tape, bring in some more ad dollars?"

I shake my head no. "Not today, Tina." I pat my pockets. "No recorder. No notes. I'm going to focus on the victims for this podcast. This is between you and me."

She turns to the side and lets out a huff, as if this bothers her, then turns back to me. "Okay. What do you want from me then?"

"It's just... why? Why did you do it?"

What she says surprises me, but I go with it. "Were you popular in high school, Johnny?"

"I wasn't prom king or the quarterback of the football team. But I did okay."

"You had a girlfriend?" she asks.

"Yeah. Linda Chun. Why?"

"Did you treat her good?"

I shrug. "You'd have to ask her about that. Most guys at that age, we're pretty immature. Linda would probably tell you the same about me."

"I wasn't very popular in high school," she says. "I didn't even have a boyfriend. Not like Lani Lum and Shayna McCarthy. They had guys falling all over them."

"Right," I say. "But Tina—"

"You have no idea how mean girls can be to each other, Johnny. Men just aren't capable of that kind of torment."

"They were mean to you in high school?"

"No. They were mean to me in middle school. By high school, I was invisible."

This seems like a poor excuse for murder to me, but I persist, because at least we're getting somewhere on a motive.

"Do you want to tell me about it?"

"They catfished me. Pretended to be a boy from another school. Got me hooked. Made me say all kinds of things. Embarrassing things, to him. And then they told everyone about how I fell for it. Showed everyone my texts. My boob pics. I wanted to die, Johnny. It was so humiliating."

"Wow, Tina. That had to hurt a lot. But what about Kimo and Derek Anderson?"

"When Kimo asked me to prom, I was on cloud nine. I had a crush on him from the time we were kids. We lived on the same block, you know. He said we were going as friends, but I got my hopes up, only to have them crushed. But years later, we reconnected. I know now that Kimo only wanted me for my family's money. I'm such a sucker.

"At first, he was great. He played the part. And when we married and moved into my family home and I got my inheritance, I didn't know enough to keep the money separate. Then he changed. And when I called him out on the cheating, he said he wanted to divorce me and take half of our wealth. After years of humiliating me. Telling me I should be grateful that he picked me. That I should shut up and put up with his side women and be glad I could call him my husband. And when I saw him chatting up Shayna McCarthy at the grocery store, I got an idea. An idea of how I could humiliate him. Ruin his reputation, and pay her back in the process."

I must admit, a different picture is starting to emerge. And I wonder. If Tina hadn't been bullied at such a tender age, would Kimo's infidelity alone have pushed her over the edge? I somehow doubt it. Maybe wounds that deep never really heal. They just scab over, leaving what's underneath to fester and stew and turn more toxic over time.

"And Derek Anderson?" I ask.

Tina rolls her eyes. "I saw him first, just like Kimo. But then I saw Derek chatting her up. That Lani Lum. I met him first, but there she was, after my guy, again. I thought after I got her out of the way, I'd have a chance with him. And I was right. But after he tried to get all kinky with me, I told him I wasn't like that. I wanted a relationship. He laughed at me and said, 'You're no Lani Lum.'

"I lost it, hearing her name. The woman Kimo picked over me. The woman Derek picked over me. She was worse than Shayna. Lani was the ringleader. I think Shayna went along with it because Lani would have turned on her if she hadn't picked on me, too. I had my gun in the car. When he insulted me, I stormed out, and he didn't try to stop me. And then I snuck in through the back door and shot him in the head. It was stupid. He was a suspect. It kept the focus off me, so I could finish what I started. If I hadn't done that ..."

She lets out a sigh, and I see where she's going with her thoughts. Tina's unhinged, that's for sure. She didn't have the smarts to get away with murder. But she's not insane. She can think straight. She'll never get off on an insanity defense.

I say, "Then I might not have come to find you."

"Yes. I might have gotten away with it," she says. "But don't worry, Johnny. I don't blame you. It was my fault. I let my emotions get the better of me. You were just trying to help."

Well, there I have it.

She's a stone-cold killer.

A stone-cold killer with a Minnie Mouse voice.

I don't need to feel too sorry for her. But the victim-centered podcasts I'm planning just got a lot more complicated. I realize, the older I get, that the lines between right and wrong, between the good people and the bad people, aren't fixed and immutable. They are fluid and contextual. This applies to me, too. And Janice. And my father, for that matter.

How far will someone go, to protect what's theirs?

To pay back a grievance?

To eliminate a threat?

We all have a breaking point, and I guess Tina reached hers.

It's best to keep that in mind, because you never know what could make a person snap.

You don't want to be someone's breaking point, that's for sure.

FORTY-TWO
JOHNNY

I've gotten a lot of answers, but one question still nags at me. I never did find out why Janice was at the police station that day. She called and said she wanted to meet with me. Here she comes now, and she still gets my heart racing.

Damn those pheromones.

We're at the same coffee shop in Kaimuki where she dumped the coffee on me. Same table, in fact. I thought it would be amusing.

She flashes me a feisty smile as she sits. "So many lovely memories, Johnny."

"I got us both iced lattes this time."

"Don't worry. I won't try and burn your balls off again. That was a one-time thing, especially after seeing what jealousy can do to a woman. Slippery slope."

"Slippery slope indeed."

"What do you think made her snap?" she asks.

"No idea," I say, although I have a better idea than most people, but I don't want to talk about that. That's not why I'm here. Plus, I'm saving it for my podcast. "She kept in close touch with the mother-in-law. That's another thing that makes this so hard to believe. Maybe that made it tougher to let go."

"Yeah I heard. That's where she got the insulin. Clever. Easy to frame Kimo that way."

"Not clever enough," I point out. "Most serial killers stay under the radar a lot longer than she did."

Janice shrugs. "You would know. So, how've you been?" she asks.

I tell her what she doesn't already know from the news reports about me, my podcast, and the case. She fills me in on her real estate career, how it's picking up a little now that interest rates have dropped. But she's studying to be an appraiser. She tells me the work is steady and reliable, even in a down market.

"I want to apologize," she says. "I shouldn't have talked you into ripping off your clients."

"I didn't have to go along with it, Janice. I made my own decision to go down that path. It's not on you. But it's nice that we both found a better way forward, even if it's not together. But I have to ask you. Do I have anything to worry about? Because I heard through the grapevine you met with some detectives at the station about Derek Anderson."

Now she looks sheepish, with that hand-in-the-cookie-jar look on her face. "About that," she says. "I did something foolish, and retaliatory. Which is another reason I wanted to meet."

"And?"

"After I figured out that you were searching up your old girlfriend, I joined a dating app. I saw Derek Anderson on it. And I went on a date with him."

"Is that how the diamond cufflinks got back into his bedroom?"

"Yeah," she says.

My stomach sinks, although I have no right to that.

I slept with Linda Chun.

I started all of it. I ruined us.

"But it's not what you think. He knew I was a real estate agent, and he was considering buying the house to use as a rental property when he returned to California. When we were chatting before we met, he mentioned that he was worried the neighborhood wasn't safe. He thought his cufflinks were stolen. I assured him he probably misplaced them. So when he asked me to look at the house and give him an idea of what I thought it could rent for, I tossed the cufflinks back behind the dresser, and then pushed one to the side of it with my foot so he'd find them. I guess he never noticed they were there. I also took a photo of those women's shoes. Just in case he was a serial killer."

"It's none of my business if you dated him, Janice."

"I guess I did it to get back at you. I knew you couldn't stand the guy, and it would stick in your gullet if I posted a photo of the two of us. But he gave me a weird vibe, even over the chats. So the day we met for coffee, I told him I got back together with my boyfriend, but I'd still be able to give him an opinion about the property. At that point, I just wanted to get in there and put the cufflinks back because I didn't want us to get busted for the break-in."

"So, about the detective interview?"

"Right. I'm getting there. Somehow, they knew I had a connection to him, so they called me in and asked me how I knew him. I don't know if they knew I met him on a dating app, but I told them that I did. I didn't want to lie. And then I told them exactly what I told you, minus the fact that I put the cuff-links back. I was shitting a brick though. I thought for sure they were going to ask me about the break-in. I guess we got away with it."

I nod, but I don't feel like I got away with anything. I think about my tarot card reading and what Marjorie said about the justice card. That I might need to make amends for something in my past before I can move forward. And even if the cards are a scam. Even if that advice could pertain to pretty much anyone, that reality rings true for me. I can't move forward and embrace the future until I fix what I did in the past, starting with Janice.

"I'm sorry too," I say. "I'm sorry about Linda Chun. How did you know?"

"I saw you a few times on your phone, looking at her social media and searching up articles about her. You're not exactly stealth. It hurt, Johnny. I mean, I thought we were good together."

"We were," I say.

We still could be.

"Then why did you do it? Why did you reach out to her?"

"I didn't. She friended me."

Janice rolls her eyes. "That's beside the point. Why did you feel the need to connect with her? Was it because I didn't want to up and move to Vegas?"

"I don't know, Janice. It was wrong. I guess what you said about the grass is greener, you were talking about her, right? And you made a good point. I reflected a lot on what you said. I miss you. And I'm sorry if I hurt you."

She looks away and then back at me. "Did you sleep with her?" she asks.

"Yes," I confess. "When she came for a visit. But we're not—"

Janice holds up a finely manicured hand. "Stop, Johnny. I don't need to know any more."

This time, she doesn't spill a drink on me. She grabs her latte and leaves, and that's probably worse. Because she still has a hold on me. And she doesn't even care enough that I slept with Linda Chun to dump a coffee on me.

Standing at the screen door, trying to decide if I should knock or ring the bell, the door opens. She's got one of those ring cameras, so I shouldn't be too surprised. She probably got it installed after we burglarized her house.

"Johnny Silva," the woman says. "I knew the Royal gave great service, but I didn't think anyone made house calls anymore. Thanks for agreeing to meet with me here."

"Hi, Agnes. It's no problem," I say.

Except that it is a problem, because there's only one reason this woman could possibly have for asking me to come over here and talk to her. But why now? Why would she confront me now? My stomach is in knots, but I fight to keep my cool.

"I love your podcast, Johnny," she says. "I'm a big fan."

"Thanks," I say, letting out a breath.

Maybe, just maybe, it's not what I think. But the sly look on her face is at odds with the compliment, so it probably is exactly what I think it is.

"Come in." Agnes steps back and invites me to walk through the doorway. "Can I get you coffee or anything?"

I decline her offer. I just want to get this over with.

"Have a seat. Please." She motions to a chair in the living area, and she takes a seat on the sofa. "Are you still working at the Royal?" she asks.

"Actually, I am, but not as a valet driver. I'm working the concierge desk three days a week. I've become a tourist attraction. The valet driver turned true crime podcaster."

"Johnny on the Spot. I love the name."

"My Uncle Mel came up with it. He's also the one who hooked me up with the cold case unit. He's a retired HPD officer."

"Do you know why you're here?" Agnes asks.

"Not really," I reply.

Except that I think I do, so I brace myself for what comes next.

"Let me tell you a little bit about me," she says. "And my marriage." Then she pauses, looking off to the side.

My trepidation turns to curiosity. Perhaps she's not right in the head, which could be good for me. Maybe she's simply a fan. A lonely older woman, looking for company. After a bit, she continues, and I let her.

"My husband was a good provider. A handsome guy. A catch, if you will. I was a real looker in my day, but being fair and blonde, I didn't age too well in the Honolulu sun. It didn't take too long for him to start straying. For years, I tried to deny it. We had a good life. Kids. I didn't want to rock the boat. If he had an occasional dalliance on a business trip, I could look the other way.

"But then about two years ago, I found a woman's earring in our bathroom. It wasn't mine, but I recognized it. It was the earring of my friend. The wife of another couple we'd known for years. I needed to know the truth. Did he bring her into our private space? The thought of it got my blood boiling. I didn't want to jump to conclusions. I needed to be sure. That's why I installed a camera in our bedroom."

Agnes eyes me, and the corners of her mouth lift to a half-smile.

My stomach lurches as the magnitude of what she's telling me sinks in. "You know," I say. "You've known? All this time?"

"I saw the video, Johnny. Yes, I know. I also know that my husband was screwing the wife of his best friend in our marital bed. But we can put that part of my story aside for now."

"I'm sorry," I say. "You were my first victim. You didn't deserve it. I broke your trust. I'm a bad person, and I have no excuse for what I did. I can pay you back for your loss. And if you want to report me, I'll confess to everything. But why didn't you do something about it back then, if you knew?"

Agnes lets out a sigh. "A couple of reasons. First, I saw your girlfriend or whoever she was going for my heirlooms. The recording doesn't have audio, but from what I could see, you told her she couldn't take those. Those were the only pieces that meant anything to me. They were passed down from my great-great-grandmother. The other pieces you grabbed were reminders of his transgressions. Every time my husband came home from a trip or a long weekend, he'd bring me these little gifts.

"It was so insulting. I was happy to be rid of the bad memories. His sorry-I-was-screwing-my-mistress consolation prizes. With the insurance money, I was able to buy myself exactly what I wanted—after I divorced him and got everything I asked for. Guilt makes a good man very malleable. You're not a bad person, Johnny. You're a person who did a bad thing, just like my husband. There's a big difference. Times are hard. People do desperate things. I led a privileged life, and you didn't. I'm happy you found a better way forward, though. Something better than resorting to petty crime. Times aren't that bad. There's always another way."

"I don't know what to say, Agnes. I'm sorry that your husband did that to you. I'm sorry I broke your trust. There must be something I can do to make amends."

"Well," she says. "I had to pay a five-hundred-dollar deductible on the insurance claim. You could cover that, now that you're doing better."

"Done," I say. "Anything else?"

"As a matter of fact, there is something else, which is another reason I asked you here. A friend of mine from back in high school. She was murdered over forty years ago. They finally solved the case a few years back. And as someone who knew a murder victim and her family, I can tell you how painful it was to not know who did it, for all those years. And she was only a friend. I can't imagine how horrible it is for a parent or a spouse or a sibling."

"Where do I come in if the case has been solved? How can I help?"

"Keep pushing forward. Solve more cold cases. If the worst thing you did was steal some rich people's jewelry, chances are all of your victims were well compensated by their insurance companies. Make up for what you did by making a difference in the world and making the most of your second chance."

I'm speechless, and there's a lump in my throat. But after I take a moment to collect myself, I tell her I need to go. And I promise to make the most of my second chance.

Not everybody will feel the way Agnes does. Take Leo, for instance. He wasn't quite so generous with his forgiveness. He agreed to be interviewed for my podcast, which allowed him to get in an *I told you so,* about Tina, which, in all fairness, he deserved.

But after we wrapped up, he said, "We're not going to be

friends, Johnny. But I'm not looking to make any trouble for you."

So, I'm going to take her advice and let myself off the hook. I've got a second chance. Everyone deserves a second chance. And I plan to make the most of it.

WHEN I GET HOME, I pull out the box that sits on the top shelf of my closet. I find the letter, the one I never opened. It's from my dad, the last one he sent, which arrived after he died. Without thinking too much about the repercussions, I slip my finger into the flap and pry it open. Then I unfold the letter and read what it says.

I'm sorry, son. Please forgive me. Not for me, but for you. I made a big mistake. Well, I made many of them. But the biggest was leaving the two of you. I loved your mom. I loved you. But I was no good for anyone back then. But I've changed. I won't ask to see you. I don't deserve it. All I ask is that you let go of the anger and resentment and get on with your life. I made some terrible choices, so don't follow in my footsteps. You're better than that. Love, Dad.

I don't know what I expected would happen when I finally read his letter. A gut-wrenching wave of emotion? A sudden burst of anger? But I don't feel any of that, because I realize that I've already forgiven my father. I've already let the anger go. Still, on some level, it feels good to finally let him speak his piece to me.

So I tuck the letter back in the box and put it back up in my closet.

And I get to work on my podcast.

FORTY-FOUR
JOHNNY

I've done a lot of interviews for this next episode, and it's taken me some serious soul searching to put it together. At first, I was convinced that Tina didn't deserve a voice. That it needed to be all about the victims. But I have to admit, when she told me about the bullying, it did change my assessment of the situation.

I'm not condoning Tina's actions, and anything Lani Lum or Shayna McCarthy did in middle school before their brains were fully matured should be excused. But it did make me think a lot about human nature. About what makes people snap. About the scars we all carry, and how we deal with them going forward.

Lani and Shayna weren't alive to defend themselves, so I asked the only person who seemed to know Tina at all. The only person who could shed some light on what had happened all those years ago. I asked Kimo's mother, Maru Fernandez, for an interview. I found it odd and curious that she and Tina had stayed close. And Maru agreed to talk to me, on the record.

Rather than make it about the women, I started out asking her about Kimo.

At first, Maru was too choked up to talk about her son. But then, as she started to tell stories about him, a smile lit up her face, like she forgot for a moment that he was no longer with us. She described him as kolohe, or rascal, a term of endearment. A cheeky, confident young man who liked to live large. He lit up a room with his charisma and his sense of humor, she said. And she had a different take on his relationship with Tina and their marriage.

Yes, she admitted. He was a ladies' man, and Tina had been the neighbor girl he grew up with. The friend he hung out with but didn't tell anyone about it, while he dated popular girls like Lani Lum, who dumped him in junior year and turned him down for prom.

Yes, Lani was a bit of a queen bee, and Shayna McCarthy was a "sweet girl," but she didn't know her very well. She didn't know the details about Tina being bullied by the two of them in middle school, but it didn't surprise her to hear that it had happened. "I have a daughter," she said. "Girls can be brutal at that age."

But she said Tina was wrong about Kimo and his feelings for her. Maru claimed that when Kimo and Tina reconnected, his affection for her was genuine, at first. He'd always cared about her, and Tina had blossomed into a very attractive woman. She'd toned up her body with exercise classes. Gotten contacts. Spruced up her wardrobe. Around Tina, Kimo could drop the false bravado and let his guard down. They'd known each other since they were seven, after all. The connection was solid, or so Maru thought.

But Tina's insecurity and jealousy turned the marriage sour. It was as if she couldn't believe that he wanted her. Yes, she had some family money, but it wasn't a fortune. Tina grew up without a dad. Her mom worked all the time or dated mister wrongs, and Maru filled in as a mother figure as best she could, which is how they had gotten close. When Tina's mom died of cancer, a few years after she and Kimo married, Tina inherited the house and the money that her mom had gotten from her parents. But that wasn't why Kimo married her, Maru said, and it wasn't worth killing anyone over.

But Tina's self-esteem hit rock bottom. No matter how much Kimo tried to convince Tina that he wasn't cheating on her, she still accused him. Followed him places. Obsessed over his social media. Threw things at him, demanding the truth. Eventually, it became a self-fulfilling prophecy, and Kimo started to stray. And then Tina got even more unhinged, and, well, we all know what happened from there.

All in all, it is a tragic cautionary tale.

So when I went to put it together, I started with Tina.

Not to glorify what she did. But to give listeners an idea of what can happen if people assume the worst of each other instead of the best. I included segments on Tina's perception of the marriage and Maru's interview to counter Tina's version of the events. I ended that segment with a comment from Maru Fernandez, imploring listeners to get help if they feel stressed, before it's too late. It was too late for Tina. Too late for Kimo, she said. But maybe not too late for the next family to not end up like theirs, mired in heartbreak and tragedy.

The segments on the other three victims followed the opening with Kimo's mom. For Shayna, I interviewed her ex, her friend Kainani, and her mother. They told a story of a hard-working and driven young woman who took AP classes and hung out with the geeks in high school. I wondered if she did that to get away from her queen bee friend, Lani Lum. Shayna was an overachiever, a straight-A student who played water polo and completed more volunteer hours than the school required. Nobody had a bad word to say about her, even the ex.

Lani Lum was represented by her coworkers and her father, who described her as a focused and driven career woman who rose to the top of a male-dominated profession and held her own at national conferences. She was slated to be in an issue of *Honolulu Magazine's* most successful women under forty. Funny, her demeanor that day she met Derek Anderson didn't match the description, and I wondered if she was as secure inside as she presented on the outside. She didn't have a boyfriend, according to my sources, but she was planning to go on a date with Derek Anderson before she died.

Derek Anderson's segment was the hardest for me, and it forced me to confront my own biases. I made a snap judgment about the guy the minute I laid eyes on him, and just because I was right, it doesn't excuse what I did. Take that woman whose cancer diagnosis I found in her glove box after she was rude to me, for example. His curtness could have been something like that. Something that had nothing to do with me.

And although Anderson was a sex freak, he wasn't doing anything illegal. He didn't force himself on Tina. Consenting adults can do what they want. So, when I put that segment together, I didn't mention the freaky parts, although it was already out there from our other podcast. I interviewed his father, who described a hard-working and driven man who dropped everything when his mother was diagnosed with Alzheimer's and got her the best care money could buy; a son and a brother, who is sorely missed by his family.

I'm not sure how this will be received by my listeners, but I feel good about the episode. As for me, I'm taking it one day at a time and trying to process everything that's happened in the last few weeks, and trying not to let the success go to my head. But I did it. I solved the case. Not bad for a valet driver.

So next time you give your keys to the valet, think of this story. Think of me. Don't think the worst, but don't let your guard down either. Be kind. Be wary. Because you never know what's going on behind a person's smile. Or what might push a reasonable person over the edge.

Take me, for example. And that guy who bit off a chunk of my earlobe at the bar in Chinatown five years ago. The one the cops brought up in the interrogation. I never thought he would do something like that, with all those people watching us. I remember it like it was yesterday. The guy was manhandling his woman that night at the dive bar, right in front of everyone. If he did that in public, who knew what he did behind closed doors?

I thought of my mother and how profoundly the abuse she witnessed affected her. The stress alone could have contributed to her cancer. I had to intervene. But I completely miscalculated the situation, and that taught me a valuable lesson. You never know how far a person will go.

He threatened me, too, and that's why I dropped the charges. Said he'd make me pay. It would have been a slam dunk in my favor. Everyone knew what he did and how he slapped his woman around in public. Turned out, she had a TRO on him, too. Lot of good that did. That wasn't his first offense, either, but it's hard to get guys like that off the street. A lot of the time, the woman won't press charges. Too scared, or brainwashed.

Still, I didn't take the bait when he tried to get me going, the few times I saw him around town. He finally gave up, which was what I was hoping for.

Because he underestimated me, too.

And my Johnny Boy smile.

He won't forget it, either. Because it's the last thing he saw when he went barreling off a cliff to his death that day, never to lay a hand on a woman again.

EPILOGUE
ONE YEAR LATER

It's been quite a year. My podcast continues to be a hit, although I never matched the kind of views I had on my first one. It's hard to top a recording of a serial killer confessing to murder. I think the only thing better would have been a live stream.

Tina's doing a life sentence without parole. Marjorie made some kind of deal and got off with a year's probation and community service, which is hard to believe, since she turned on me at the end. She claims that Tina showed up at her house with some sob story about Kimo being a serial killer, but over time, a different picture started to emerge. Marjorie went along with it because she thought Tina would kill her too, and that I can believe. There wasn't a trial, so I was spared the stress of testifying. But I did give them my statement and my recording, which they used to extract the confession.

Meanwhile, I'm Johnny on the Spot, the valet driver turned true crime podcaster, an inspiration, it seems. Living proof that you can go from a minimum wage job to crushing it in the creator economy. I don't want to think about what a long shot it was, and how hard it's going to be to keep it going. That's why I'm still at the Royal three days a week, working the concierge desk or the valet if they need me, signing the occasional request for an autograph. It's good to have a backup plan. And then there's that great health insurance.

My latest cold case is a heartbreaking one. An eight-year-old foster child who went missing in the nineties and was never found. The little guy didn't just up and leave town, but he has nobody to speak for him or press the case. The parents are MIA. The foster parents were suspects but never charged. His tutu tried for years to get them to work the case, but she died two years ago. It's a long shot, but I'm working it hard.

And now, I've got an inside look at the cold cases that come into the unit, and I'm happy to report that the guy who bit off a chunk of my earlobe is not even on the list. His death was ruled an accident, and if that ever changes, I'll be the first to know. I doubt it will, though. I was very careful to cover my tracks that day, and I'm betting on the fact that the cops won't care too much about a scumbag like him.

Believe it or not, I haven't dated at all. I ended up going to a few AA meetings. I don't think I'm addicted to weed, but I wasn't comfortable with the hold it had on me. I picked AA because it seemed better than Narcotics Anonymous. I'm not doing anything illegal.

My dad went to AA for a while, during the period when he was trying to get in touch with me. Before he started drinking again and drove himself into a tree. I knew about the amends, the way you're supposed to take responsibility for your actions.

He tried to do that with me, but I wouldn't let him, which I realize now was pretty immature. I knew about the twelve steps and the higher power. The program isn't for me in the long term, but I gained a lot from the few meetings I attended. One thing they suggest is that, while you're trying to get your act together, you should avoid starting a new relationship.

I thought it was good advice. But I'm in a better place now, and it's been a year. That's why I'm headed to see Linda Chun. I'm at a podcaster conference in San Francisco, and when she saw on my social media that I was here, she hit me up, letting me know she was here too, visiting a friend.

I still feel bad about the way we left things, so Linda will be my final amends. It seemed mutual, though. She didn't try very hard to stay in touch with me either. I have to give her credit, too. Because once I got somewhat famous with the podcasts, she didn't try to muscle in and capitalize on it like the many other people who came out of the woodwork.

She greets me at the door to her suite, looking LA hot. Truthfully, I kind of liked her better as an island girl. After we get the pleasantries out of the way, she pours us some white wine and ushers me out to the balcony. She's staying near the Embarcadero, and there's a great view of the Bay Bridge. The balcony is small and cozy and surprisingly private in this corner unit.

"I'm sorry I wasn't in touch more," I say. "Things were so crazy when you were visiting. And everything happened so fast between us. I hope I didn't push you into anything you weren't ready for."

She laughs. "Johnny. I'm not a teenager anymore. And I'm the one who stopped texting you. I'm the one who should apologize to you. But you see, it wasn't what I thought it was going to be, being intimate with you again. You know what I mean?"

Well, this is a shocker. I thought I was the one who blew her off. But damn if it doesn't make me want her a little more, and I can't help but wonder if she's playing some kind of game with me. After all, she contacted me to meet up. She's been keeping tabs on me, not the other way around.

My brow furrows as I size her up. "And that's why you wanted to meet? To apologize?"

"Well, that, and I thought you might be able to help me tell my side of the story, since you're a podcaster now. Since you know what it's like to be unfairly accused of murder." Linda stands, leaning her back against the balcony railing, twirling her wine glass in her hand. Then she turns from me to admire the view. "Look at this. It's spectacular," she says. "Don't you think? Come. Have a look."

"I don't like heights," I say.

She trails her fingers over the white metal railing. "You'll be fine. Just don't look down."

Not wanting to seem like a wuss, I get up and stand next to her, and we both gaze off in the distance, facing the bay.

She says, "That is so weird that Tina was holding a grudge from high school. Can you imagine?"

"I can't," I admit. "Seems a little crazy to me."

"Yeah. Like, I don't care that you cheated on me with Maile Kahele the night of senior prom."

I turn toward her. "What are you talking about?"

"Johnny." She bats me on the arm, wearing a half-smile. "It's fine. I'm not angry. We were kids."

"I didn't cheat on you with Maile Kahele," I say.

"You didn't?"

"No. Where did you get that idea?"

"A friend. You're telling me that nothing at all happened between you and Maile Kahele, the night of our senior prom?"

Something did happen with Maile, and I'm suddenly aware of the fact that I'm twenty stories up. A dash of vertigo hits me, and I feel like she already knows.

"Okay," I confess. "We made out a little. I was drunk. You were pissed at me about something, and you stormed off. But I didn't sleep with her, I swear."

Not at prom, anyway.

"Well, that's something, I guess. Thanks for being honest with me. After what I've been through, I can't deal with any more lies."

"What you've been through?"

"My husband, Rob."

"It must have been hard, losing him in that way," I say, but I don't get the connection, or why she's bringing him up now, in this context.

"It was," she says. "Watching him struggle and writhe in the churning water, seeing his head bob up and down until it didn't anymore."

"You tried to save him," I say, as my stomach twists. "You did what you could."

A sly grin spreads across her face. "Yes. But you see, he was cheating on me, too. So I didn't try very hard."

Before she can hurl me off the balcony, I push her aside, dash across the hotel suite, and barrel out the door with the force of a hurricane.

As I head for the staircase, I hear her laughing her head off as she calls out to me: "I'm just messing with you, Johnny. Johnny! Come back!"

And as I'm racing down the stairs, taking them two by two, a thought flashes into my mind, and I feel like knocking myself upside the head:

I wonder what Janice is up to these days.

Janice and me, we were great together.

Maybe Janice is the one...

ACKNOWLEDGMENTS

My sincere thanks to the many people who helped me craft this novel and bring it to completion.

Thanks to my invaluable alpha readers Rick, Robin, and Susan who offered excellent suggestions and encouragement. Thanks to Christina Yother for her keen editorial insights. Thanks to all of my advance copy readers on Booksprout and NetGalley who take the time to read my books and post their reviews. Thanks to fellow thriller authors Caleb Stephens, Scott Kikkawa, R.G. Belsky, Douglas Corleone, Jennifer Sadera, and Jennifer van der Kleut for their beta reads, blurbs, support, encouragement, and camaraderie. Please check out their fabulous thriller and mystery novels.

Thanks to Honolulu, my adopted hometown, for all the great memories that I will forever cherish and the friends I've made who are like family to me now. I stopped in Honolulu decades ago when I was in my twenties on a year-long trip around the world. I decided to stay a little longer than I'd planned, so long that I now have two grandchildren, both born in Honolulu within the last year and a half.

With this novel, I hope to bring this vibrant, multi-cultural city to life and give readers a glimpse of why I love it here so much. Times are tough, though, and the price of paradise is steep and getting steeper. There are no easy answers, and not everyone will make it as a true crime podcaster, like Johnny. Also, please know that I valet my car without hesitation all over this town. This story and the hotel where it is set are pure fiction, just like my dating app thriller, which I wrote even though I met my husband online, and so did my daughter. But still, if you can afford it, a decent tip and a kind word are always appreciated, I would imagine, wherever you happen to be.

Finally, thanks so much to my readers. You are why I keep writing, and I am so grateful for the time you take to read my books as well as rate and comment on them. I read all of my reviews, and they help me improve, so please keep them coming. I really appreciate it.

For updates, book reviews, and special offers, please go to www.bonnietraymore.com and sign up for my quarterly newsletter.

ABOUT THE AUTHOR

Bonnie Traymore is the award-winning, Amazon charts bestselling author of domestic and psychological thrillers. Her books feature complex, relatable protagonists who find themselves in extraordinary circumstances. She lives in Honolulu with her family.

On the following pages, please enjoy a sample of *The Rich Guy's Wife: A Twisty Domestic Thriller*. Erin has always dreamed of a life of luxury. But at what price?

PROLOGUE

Mother's voice rings in my ears as I stand perfectly still in the darkness, fearing that each breath I take will be my last:

Be careful what you wish for, Erin.

I'm crouched down in the closet, my legs and back aching to move, even an inch. But I can't. One twitch, one cramp, and I'll bang into a shelf and give myself away.

Sweat beads form at my hairline, nagging at me as they threaten to drip down my face. I slide a hand up my side, being careful not to bang into anything, and wipe away the dampness. Perspiration mixes with the blood on my hand, reminding me of the carnage outside the door.

Why did I touch the body?

I always thought my mother said things like that to darken my dreams. To stave off the inevitable disappointment that comes from shooting too high in life and falling short. For daring to reach for the stars, only to have them slip through your fingers and fall away like glitter from a magic wand.

Nothing she said deterred me, though. Because I figured something out pretty early on in life. In New York City, if you're not filthy rich, you're poor—and I was not going to end up like her.

But I see now that my mother spoke from experience.

She knew them.

Studied them.

Understood them.

The rich guys, and their wives.

What she really meant was:

Be careful what you're wishing for, Erin.

Because I got what I wished for.

I'm a rich guy's wife now.

And it just might be the death of me.

CHAPTER ONE

ERIN

It's one of those magical Friday nights in Manhattan, full of hope and possibilities. It's nearly seven in the evening, and we're on the brink of summer, but a slight nip in the air remains. Soon, the summer swelter will arrive, dividing the haves and the have-nots, turning the city into a ghost town as far as the who's who and filling it with twenty-year-old college interns, out-of-town tourists, and bridge and tunnel weekend warriors. In short, time is running out.

I enter the bar guardedly optimistic, which is pretty much my go-to state. At heart, I'm an optimist, but that's been tempered over the years by my upbringing and life experiences. Still, a little uptick in my pulse tells me that hope lives in me, and as I search the crowd for my friend Lucy, I can't help but notice that the ratio is in our favor this evening.

Bumping up against a pack of twenty-something giggly girls, already tipsy but young enough to come off looking cute rather than pathetic, my biological clock ticks like a time bomb. I've been at this for far too long. At some point, I'll have to settle. Or move. Or something. At thirty-one, I still have some time, but not much.

"Hey, Erin," Lucy calls out, her hand shooting up from her perch at the bar.

We're aiming for the after-work crowd tonight. Lucy Chang is a star defense attorney, the kind who doesn't need a man to live large. We met in private school, lost touch, and then reconnected. Her dark, silky hair shimmers in the wash of the overhead lights. She's dressed in a gray pencil skirt and a soft white blouse, unbuttoned just enough to add a hint of sexy to her toughness.

I'm wearing a cobalt blue dress that hugs my body and brings out my eyes. Not too short, just above the knee, but with little slits on the sides that hint at what's underneath. We make good barfly partners, the two of us. The tall, thin brunette and the busty blonde.

"What'll you have?" she asks, snapping her fingers at the bartender.

The bartender glares at Lucy as he positions himself in front of me. He's cute. Really cute. But he's not the kind of guy I'm looking for. Still, he's a human being, and Lucy can be a little harsh sometimes. Plus, I don't want him to poison us.

"Sorry about my friend," I say to him with a smile. "She spends her days with hardened criminals."

"Guilty." Lucy offers an apologetic shrug.

He smiles back at me. "What can I get you?" he asks me.

"A champagne cocktail," I reply.

Lucy's saved me a seat, but it's three-deep at the bar and standing room only now. It's a large bar in a trendy restaurant. Koho, it's called. Just east of Grand Central, so we'll get the Westchester commuter crowd, too. We catch up as we scan the room, pretending that we're there to gal pal when it's obvious we're here to meet guys. If we really wanted to talk, we'd do lunch or go for a power walk.

Next to us are a pair of elder statesmen. They must be close to fifty, or even older. Divorcées, if I had to guess, from the way they're looking around, not talking to one another. Or married guys in search of a little on the side. I'm not attracted to men that age, and although my goal is to marry money, I'm not about to force myself into anything that doesn't feel right on a physical level. I'm not that desperate. I'll never be that desperate.

Lucy and I catch each other up on our happenings as we sip our cocktails and try not to look too available. She tells me about her latest case, a supposed whistleblower who it turns out was embezzling from his company and is now facing criminal charges. We pass the time, but my heart's not in it. I'm tired, and I think about reviving my online dating profile. I needed a break, but looking at the drink prices, a monthly subscription probably offers more bang for the buck.

I'm about to tell Lucy we should call it a night when I notice a guy standing in the corner, checking me out. He's alone, it seems. Wearing a suit and tie, which makes him stand out—in a good way. Frankly, I'm not a big fan of the dressing down trend. His dark gray suit jacket hangs perfectly on his broad shoulders, obviously tailor-made. A blue-and-white-striped tie sits on a starched white collared shirt. His face is serious and symmetrical. Handsome—and young enough for me.

I turn away, not wanting to make it obvious that I'm interested in him. Maybe he's not looking at me, in particular. The older guys next to me ask if they can buy us a drink, but I respectfully decline, although the drinks are so expensive here, I'll probably only be able to have two over the course of the evening.

Turning back to Lucy, I see that she's busy chatting with

the guy next to her, so I sneak a glance back in Suit Guy's direction. His pressed lips curl up to a smile, letting me know that he knows I'm interested. He starts strolling in my direction, and I feel a little flutter in my stomach.

At least I think he's coming toward me, but now I can't see him through the crowd. After a few minutes, I spot him talking to one of the giggly girls. She's holding him by the arm, and his back is to me. It seems he's been intercepted. If he's looking for a hook-up, she's probably a better bet. Those days are over for me.

Oh well.

Lucy asks me if I want another drink.

I tell her I'm not sure.

A tap on my shoulder pulls my attention from her.

"I'd like to get that for you," a voice says as I turn around.

Suit Guy has a faint accent.

European.

Probably German, which explains the suit and tie.

"I'm Stefan," he says.

Well, I'll let him buy me a drink, but this isn't going to be the man of my dreams. I'm not about to play tour guide for some foreign guy looking for an escort during his business trip. But still, he seems nice enough, so I say yes to the drink.

"I'm Erin," I say. "And this is my friend Lucy."

When he smiles, his stoic exterior softens. I have to admit, Stefan is having an effect on me, in spite of myself. It's a little noisy in the bar now, and we have to strain to carry on a conversation. Lucy busies herself talking to the guy next to her, although I'm pretty sure she's not interested in him. She's a good wing woman.

Stefan keeps the focus on me, asking me questions about myself. I'm very selective about what I disclose in these kinds of situations. I work in marketing, I say, keeping it short and sweet.

If he asks, I'll reveal that I attended an exclusive private high school, followed by a prestigious liberal arts college for undergrad. I won't disclose that I was a scholarship student at both institutions. Erin Donovan, daughter of Mary Donovan, a single mother who worked two jobs that barely covered our rent.

But he doesn't ask much about my past. Rather, he asks me what I like to do. I tell him I'm more of an indoor cat, preferring museums and gallery openings to hikes and nature adventures. He smiles at this. A slightly crooked smile that makes him look less serious, more fun.

Up close, he's even more handsome than he was from far away. His twinkly eyes are dark hazel with a hint of blue, or perhaps that's the overhead light bouncing off my dress. I think he has the kind of eyes that change color depending on the setting. His jaw is square, his face angular and strong. Lips full, but not too full, and totally kissable.

Too bad he's not from here.

Stefan is a tad cagey about himself, not really answering my question when I ask what he does. "I'm in commodities," he says.

Is he a trader? Does he own an oil rig? Is he intentionally being vague to seem more intriguing? Whatever it is, it's working. The second champagne cocktail is loosening me up, and I can't believe I'm actually considering a one-night stand with this guy. Even though he's not marriage material, it's been months since my last relationship, and I have to admit, I miss the feel of a man's hands on my body. He smells good, too. A hint of aftershave mixed with man scent.

"Where do you live?" I ask, expecting something like Hamburg, Brussels, or Zurich.

"The Hamptons," he says. "Would you like to get out of here and grab some dinner? My driver's outside."

My eyes widen, and he gives me that closed-lip smile again. I try hard to dampen my enthusiasm, but I fail miserably. A giddy grin spreads up my face. He knows I'm going to say yes and so do I, even though the guy could be a serial killer, for all I know.

"Sure," I say. "I'd love to have dinner with you. But why don't we stay here and get a table? I'm not in the habit of getting into cars with strangers."

"Fair enough," Stefan says. "But we're not going to be strangers for very long."

To find out if Stefan is Erin's dream guy or her worst nightmare, check my website for retail information at bonni etraymore.com.

www.ingramcontent.com/pod-product-compliance
Lightning Source LLC
Chambersburg PA
CBHW060352310726
48976CB00003B/796